Down the Long Stairs

WINIFRED CAWLEY

Down the Long Stairs

ILLUSTRATED BY

WILLIAM STOBBS

London
OXFORD UNIVERSITY PRESS
1974

Oxford University Press, Ely House, London W. 1

GLASGOW NEW YORK TORONTO MELBOURNE WELLINGTON
CAPE TOWN IBADAN NAIROBI DAR ES SALAAM LUSAKA ADDIS ABABA
DELHI BOMBAY CALCUTTA MADRAS KARACHI LAHORE DACCA
KUALA LUMPUR SINGAPORE HONG KONG TOKYO

ISBN 0 19 272054 6

Printed in Holland
Zuid-Nederlandsche Drukkerij N.V.
's-Hertogenbosch

FOREWORD

This story is set against the background of the Second Civil War which took place in 1648 and was one part of the long struggle between King Charles I and Parliament.

Some of the characters who appear or are mentioned were actual historical personages. These are always minor characters in the story, though major ones in the history of Newcastle and Northumberland at that time. Such are Sir Arthur Hazelrigg, Governor for Parliament of Newcastle; Lieutenant-Colonel Henry Lilburne, Deputy-Governor of Tynemouth Castle; Sir Marmaduke Langdale, Commander of the Royalist forces in the Northern Counties; and, of course, the great Oliver Cromwell himself.

The military and political events which form the background of the story are also historically true. Sieges, troop movements, major battles, and minor skirmishes can all be authenticated from contemporary sources, of which the most important is the *Historical Collections* of John Rushworth, at one time assistant Clerk to the House of Commons and in 1648 Secretary to Lord Fairfax, Commander in Chief of the Parliamentary army. The only troop movement in the story I have invented is the evacuation of Cartington Castle by the Roundheads. Yet I have invented it only in the sense that I have not found a precise reference to it. It *could* have happened and possibly did.

The general background is as true as I could make it after intensive reading of Guild records, old diaries (astonishingly there are a number of seventeenth-century diaries still in existence), early engineering accounts of coal-mining, old books on behaviour, medical books, recipe books, accounts of travels, household accounts—all the detritus of history which can be more fascinating than history itself.

The major events of the story, the adventures of Ralph Cole, son of a Royalist, stepson of a Roundhead, are imaginary. So are all the major characters. Yet they also are, in a sense, true, for I believe that *all* the things that happened to Ralph were happening to people in Newcastle and Northumberland in 1648 and all the people he met might have been found there.

Chapter 1

The hollow between sleep and waking was warm and safe. Far away St. Nicholas's clock struck. Unnumbered, the chimes sank down among the half-thoughts that as yet scarcely stirred in my brain. Sleep still shut me out of myself: I had no past, no future, scarcely a name.

It was no use: there was already too much effort in my inactivity. I half-opened my eyes: the light was still grey and woollen. I closed them again. For a moment longer I let sleep shut out the present, but it was only for a moment: already I knew that I must wake up and become Ralph Cole again.

Then I heard feet on the stairs: heavy, confident feet, and quiet, careful feet. Now I certainly must awake. If Lieutenant

Harbottle Grimston and Captain Sydrach Simpson were coming to bed after their night patrol, I had already slept too long. The noltherd's horn blew from close at hand, the slippery clatter of cattle on cobbles came from below my window: I should have been up half an hour ago.

The feet were near the top of the stairs now. The misery which had been aching at the back of my mind gave way to anger—anger with the men because I had been compelled to share my room with them, anger with myself for being caught in the room and not yet dressed. I had from the very first day decided that if I stayed in the room with them a single unnecessary moment, I should be making friends with the King's enemies.

They were talking when they reached the landing: Sydrach Simpson in a low voice, Harbottle Grimston (I rejected their Parliament-given titles) in loud, assertive tones that refused to make any concessions to the peace of a delinquent household.

Simpson softly pushed open the door and Grimston clumped in before him. Simpson was a tall man, but slender and surprisingly—for a Roundhead—quiet and gentle. Grimston was equally tall, but big-boned and heavy, loud-voiced, and certainly not gentle. They had not expected to see me still there, and surprise snapped the thread of their talk. I was immediately sure they had been saying something that they did not want me to hear. I was only fifteen, and ready to believe my affairs the most interesting topic of conversation in the world. Mind you, at that particular moment I had some justification for my sensitiveness. Without a doubt, the affairs of the Coles, the Nicholas Coles, *were* being talked over that day in most of the merchant families of Newcastle, for they had just taken a turn surprising enough to oust, for a while at least, from conversation, the phenomenal price of corn, the unseasonable cold and wet, the movements of the Scottish army and the possibility of a new siege of Newcastle, even the wearying delay of Lieutenant-General Cromwell in coming to help Lambert to hold the North for Parliament. They were even interesting enough to make hostmen forget—for a moment—the state of the coal trade.

The hooks of my doublet seemed twice as numerous and half as docile as usual. I kept my head down and pretended that I had not heard Sydrach Simpson's civil 'Good morning': he

2

did not repeat it. I heard the rattle of his bandoleer as he took it off and put it on the stool between his bed and mine. Harbottle Grimston sat down on the edge of his bed and began pulling off his great, ugly army shoes. I had never looked at him from such close quarters before. All I could see were his shoes, his grey breeches, and the skirt of his scarlet coat. It struck me with surprise that he was shabby, and his shoes, in spite of their polish, looked worn and cracked. Well, he probably had not been paid for months. Serve him right, the dirty Roundhead, I thought. My mother had not been paid either, for providing him with quarters and food.

I took my gaze away from him; I must hurry if I did not want to get caught in one of his interminable prayers. He was sure to pray before going to bed, and if I were there, he would certainly pray for me and my stubbornness, with loud references to sons of Belial and frogs of the bottom-most pit that would be even harder to bear than usual that morning.

At last: the final hook caught. I snatched my handkerchief from under my pillow and was out on the landing and half-way down the stairs before my real thoughts began crowding in at last.

There was no one on the stairs and only Alyse in the kitchen, which was strange, for our house was sadly overcrowded these days. Alyse had her back to me, and was clearing away the remains of the officers' supper, or was it everyone else's breakfast?

'Alyse, where is everybody?' I asked.

'Oh, Master Ralph, you fairly made me jump,' she said. 'They've all eaten and gone. It's long past five o'clock, but your mother said not to call you. She's in the counting-house and wants to see you later on.'

'Where's Emmet?' I asked.

'She's gone with Cousin Barbary up to the markets to watch the Fair folks making ready for selling off and . . .' she broke off. She was very short-sighted these days but now she was near enough to get a good look at me.

'Now, Ralph, what will Mistress Cole say if she sees you like that?' She clucked around me, pulling my bands straight, smoothing my hair.

'She won't even notice, like as not,' I muttered, and all my misery, set free at last, rushed to my throat; 'and if she does, she won't care.'

Alyse sighed. 'Now, Ralph lad, it's no good starting all over again: we had enough last night. You'll just have to make the best of it. That's what poor Mistress Cole has had to do.'

So Alyse had accepted it already. My mother was 'poor Mistress Cole' and soon it would be 'Mistress Trumbell'. Trumbell ... if the man had even had a less ridiculous name, I swore to myself, I should have minded him less.

'But, Alyse, how *could* she? How could she? Thomas Trumbell, of all people, my father's own factor.'

Alyse had been my mother's nurse as well as mine and Emmet's. She had thought even Nicholas Cole hardly good enough for the daughter of Sir George Selby. The Coles were rich enough, but much newer folk than the Selbys. How could she bear the thought of Thomas Trumbell so calmly then? Thomas Trumbell. The name stuck in my throat.

'Now, Ralph,' said Alyse in her 'let's have no more nonsense' voice, 'Master Trumbell ...' (So it was *Master* Trumbell now, was it? It used to be plain Thomas.) 'is a sober, decent man, and well thought of by the Parliament men. He can make things a lot easier for your mother.'

'Aye, and even with what's left, Mother can make things a lot easier for him,' I replied furiously.

'That remains to be seen,' Master Ralph,' she said. 'There's many a man these days would think twice about marrying the widow of a known King's man.'

There was truth in what she said, but that only made me more determined still not to see reason.

'Well, anyway, she might have thought about Emmet and me,' I said.

'That's just what she *is* doing,' said Alyse with an infuriating air of patience. She paused for a moment, then went on, 'We were on the wrong side last time. Well,' she concluded with satisfaction, 'this time it won't matter to us who wins or loses.'

The wrong side. How could she call the King's side that? If she thought these arguments would reconcile me to my mother's projected marriage to the family factor she could not have been more mistaken. She was just saying exactly what I was afraid everyone else would be saying—that my mother's new marriage would bring certain very practical advantages with it. Alyse approved of it, therefore. She was an old woman and had not liked watching the declining fortunes of the family which she had served all her life and whose wealth and prestige she thought more important than a few principles. My mother apparently felt the same: she had more or less said so the previous night when she had told Emmet and me that she intended to marry Thomas Trumbell.

I do not think I was capable, just then, of disentangling all the strands of my feelings. If I had been, I think that probably I should have found that a powerful part of my resentment was a fear that I had been made to look a fool, and on two counts. In the first place, I had often boasted to my friends and at school about my Royalist connexions, particularly about my mother's family, the Selbys, and now she was going to marry a man known throughout Newcastle as a supporter of Parliament. In the second place, the man she had chosen was not even a member of one of the few good Newcastle families who had opposed the King, but one of those new men who had made their principles profitable. This same Thomas Trumbell had, only this summer, set the whole town talking when he had been admitted to the Hostmen's Guild, which he never would have been, had not Sir Arthur Hazelrigg, the Governor of Newcastle appointed by Parliament, brought pressure to bear on the Guild. I felt that I could never face either my friends or my enemies again.

It was small wonder then that the night before I had received the news my mother gave me with a storm of incredulous abuse, in which I had blamed her for every bad moment I had ever known, until poor, white-faced Emmet, who had been summoned with me, burst into tears, and my mother had ordered me to bed immediately and without any supper, like a naughty boy, not like a young man of fifteen. I had managed to keep my tears back until I was upstairs. Fortunately I had my room to myself at night. If the men who were quartered on us, two of them in my room, had not been on the night watch of the walls and water-gates, there would not have been a corner of the house where I could have had my cry out alone.

No one had come near me: obviously my mother was very angry and had ordered both Alyse and Emmet to stay away from me. I was glad of this at first, but by the time I had stopped crying I should have been glad to see either of them, and grew angry again, because they, like the rest of the world, were against me. I had been sent supperless to bed on other occasions, but never until then had Alyse or Emmet failed to smuggle me something to eat.

That was the first night in my life that I could not get to sleep for the thoughts that kept churning round and round in my head and would not let me be. I heard the sounds of the house settling down for the night and I grew wider and wider awake. That was the first time I had been miserable alone. When my father was killed, we had all shared one sorrow and, besides, our grief was blunted by terror of what the Scots would do to the captured city—terror which made us cling together. Now I had the feeling that I was in a house where familiar, friendly faces had turned strange and unkind, and where life had been wrenched off its old, safe lines, and might run anywhere, like the truck I had seen, only the previous week, cause so much damage down at the staithes.

Yet I must have dropped off to sleep at last. I could remember counting St. Nicholas's chimes all the hours until one. Whether I had heard any more before those that woke me I could not be sure. 'You'll be better in the morning,' Alyse always used to say to Emmet or me when we had any aches or pains, and we usually were, but this morning it was different. I felt as miserable as I had done the night before. And I was still in disgrace, I told myself. Everybody was keeping out of my way. Even Alyse was against me: I had counted on her—and on Emmet. They had both let me down. All right, I was on my own now. I would show them all. . . .

'Now, come on, Ralph, get on. There's plenty to be done today and I can't get a start till these pots are out of the way,' said Alyse, briskly.

She had set down some bread and cheese beside my morning ale and I was hungry after my supperless night, but I pointedly ate only a mouthful of bread and pushed the rest aside. To my disappointment, Alyse scarcely seemed to notice.

'Well, if you've had what you want, you'd better go and see your mother, Ralph,' she said. 'She left word you were to go to the counting-house as soon as you were ready.'

I wished I had taken longer over my breakfast.

'Now, come on, Ralph: it's no good hanging back. Go and

get it over with like a good lad.' The softening in her voice touched the edge of the hard lump of misery inside me; but she went on, 'And mind you say you're sorry.'

I had never been good at that, even when I *had* something to ask pardon for. Self-pity and hurt pride hardened again and by the time I was stumping along the passage to the counting-house, I had made up my mind that I would say as little as possible to my mother—nothing at all, if that could be managed —and, under no circumstances was I going to apologize. My mother had told me, in effect, to mind my own business. All right, I would. I would never mention Thomas Trumbell again, and I would never speak to him, either. I prided myself on my ability to be the last to give way in a quarrel. True, so far, I had only set myself against Emmet, or Jamesie Selby or Cousin Barbary, or boys at school, but it ought to be no harder with my mother: I never saw much of her, anyway. So I told myself, but my treacherous courage threatened to fail me as I raised my hand to knock at the office door. At heart, I was afraid of my mother. It was Alyse who had really brought up Emmet and me. After my father was killed, my mother had been too busy to spare us much time. We thought her hard: perhaps she was. But life cannot have been easy for her, and she had done what some men had failed to do: she had kept the wreck of the family business afloat during the worst period the coal trade had ever known.

I can still remember that I paused, and that my breath quavered a little, and my knuckles were loth to rap on the door. What if Thomas Trumbell were there? No, he could not be. This was one of the busiest times of the year: even this year, when fewer foreign traders than usual had come to the Lammas Fair, for fear that the new war would close the Tyne and stop the coal trade as the first war had, four years ago, there was still plenty for Trumbell and his assistant to do, running back and forwards between pits and staithes, between the Custom-House and the Town Chamber, and dealing with keelmen and pit overmen, and impatient shipmasters and suspicious collectors of taxes. During this strange summer my mother had sent me with him on several occasions, but only inside the city walls. As Newcastle waited, almost hourly, a new siege, this time by the King's forces, Emmet and I had not been allowed out of the city gates. My mother thought I might as well be starting to learn something of a hostman's business, for I was to be apprenticed in the autumn. So I had gone with Trumbell and I had liked him well enough then: but I refused to remember that now.

At last I knocked on the door. My mother's voice called me in. She was alone: the moment when I should have to greet Thomas Trumbell in our new relationship was postponed. She was sitting at her counter, checking a stack of returned cockets against a list propped up in front of her. She did not look up. It never occurred to me that she might be as nervous as I was; if I had thought anything at all, it would have been that she was, as usual, too busy to deal with me straight away.

She came to the end of the cockets and arranged them in their box, which she locked before putting it away. At last she turned to me and gave me a formal good morning which I returned with equal formality. I waited, wondering whether she would refer to last night's scene. Her face was as calm and unreadable as always. There was a moment's silence.

'This morning, Ralph, I want you to take a message to the salt-pans at Shields.' I was surprised and even suspicious. Emmet and I had nagged in vain all summer to be allowed outside the walls. Why was I being allowed to go so far afield now? My mother went on, 'Jackie Armstrong will take you. He's got a keel of pan-coals to take down. Tell Will Reaveley to let the fire out under eight of the pans. Since the Colchester boats haven't come this summer, we cannot get rid of all the salt. There's no point in wasting coal and wages piling up salt we can't sell. Tell him to lay off one of the men: I don't care which one it is. Is that clear?'

I nodded, without saying anything. She hesitated, obviously about to say more. Then, in a slightly quicker voice, she went on, 'After that, go to the Shields jetty and wait for Master Trumbell. He'll be there about an hour before noon.'

So that was it. I was to have my first meeting with Master Trumbell in a public place, where all eyes would be upon us. I could just imagine my mother saying, 'He'll have to behave himself there. And after the first time it'll be easier.' Well, that would not work, I told myself: I'd get out of it somehow. As one part of me was thinking these thoughts, another part was listening to my mother saying, 'Master Trumbell has to go to the Billy Pit. He'll take you with him. You've never been there before, have you? The coal's poor, but it's good enough for our assessment for Tynemouth Castle.'

Now that Trumbell's name had been mentioned and I had said nothing, her voice slowed on to its natural pace:

'Tell the overman to send ten wagon-loads less to the pans each week from now on. And tell him to send the ten wagon-loads to the Castle instead. I expect they'll grumble about the quality of it, but it's good enough to give away.'

It was not like my mother to give me so many explanations. For the first time I began to think that she was as nervous as I was: even more so, maybe. But this did not make me soften towards her—all my pity was for myself—instead, it made me feel more self-righteous than ever.

She was smoothing out the lists on her counter. Then she stood up, and looking straight at me at last, said, in a tone that rejected any possibility of argument, 'You will be civil to Master Trumbell this morning, and this evening, too, when he takes supper with us and with your uncle.'

She was as hard as ever. How could I have thought, even for a moment, that she could soften? She gave me no chance to speak, but picking up a paper, handed it to me.

'Here is your pass for leaving the city and for getting in again this afternoon.' I took it without a word and put it, without looking at it, into my pocket. 'You would have done better to see for yourself that it's in order,' she said. 'You leave too much to other people, Ralph, for all you think you're a man now.' She finally reduced me to boyhood again by adding, 'And, Ralph, you'll wear your old buff doublet, and breeches, and your oldest cloth hose and shoes. Those things you've got on are far too good to go round the pans, or to the pithead. Now you'd better go: it's late already.'

Trust my mother to think of taking care of my clothes, even at such a time. On any other day I might have protested about having to change my clothes, but on this particular day I was too angry. Even if I had not sworn to myself that I would keep silent, I was so furious now that I durst not trust my voice.

My mother turned again to her papers. I was dismissed.

Ever since my mother had taken over the many ramifications of my father's affairs, she and I had grown further and further apart, until we scarcely knew how to talk to each other. Then this year when I was fifteen, she had decided to initiate me gradually to the family business before I was finally bound apprentice to my father's old friend, Sir Francis Anderson, and we had come a little closer. Now we were further apart than ever, and it was all her fault, or so I believed. Looking back after all these years, I do not see how she could have acted differently. After my father's death, his affairs were in a sorry state. Much of his money was in various branches of the coal trade, which, because of the war, had been almost at a standstill during the last months of his life, for the Tyne had been blockaded by Parliament. Some of our mines had been drowned that summer of 1644—many of the miners had been pressed into the Scottish and Roundhead armies to serve as sappers against the walls of Newcastle, and there had not been enough men left to keep the mines free from water. Even in 1648 some of the mines were still producing nothing and would need large sums of money spent on them to put them in working order again. Staithes, wagon-ways, salt-pans belonging to us had suffered severe damage. Then again, my father had loyally subscribed large sums towards maintaining the Royalist garrison in Newcastle. The final blow had come after he had been killed in the storming of the city by the Scots, for a large fine had been levied against his estate by the local Committee of Parliament. My mother had had to fend for herself. Her brothers and cousins were known Royalists and either had fled over the water like my father's kin or were crippled by new anti-Royalist regulations. As a hostman's widow, she had been allowed by the Guild to carry on my father's business. Parliament had tried at first to exclude Royalists from the coal trade, but the south country's need of coal was desperate and they had very soon had to come round to letting experienced coal-owners carry on, even if they *were* delinquents, though the conditions under which Royalist coal was compelled to be sold were well-nigh crippling. It was not easy even for Parliament men during those unsettled days: for a woman, watched and penalized at every turn for her Royalist connexions, to have kept her head above water was, I see now, nothing short of miraculous. I must have added to her difficulties, a sulky boy resenting her inevitable neglect of Emmet and me, fancying myself a champion of the cause for which my father had died and thinking that by being insolent to Parliament men and, especially, to the soldiers who were always being quartered on us, I was somehow being brave for Charles Stuart's sake. I thought she was hard: the wonder is that she was not harder. I wish I had had a better chance later to show her that I was sorry for all the trouble I caused her.

So it came about that on the morning of 9 August, in the year of Our Lord 1648, I left my home in the Close. Alyse's parting words had been those she had been using every day for I could not remember how long: 'Good-bye, Ralph. Be a good boy, and mind you come straight home.' Did she think I was going to school? Would she never realize I had grown up?

I was wearing my oldest clothes, and carrying over my shoulder a knapsack of bread, cheese, and slices of dried neat's tongue. In my purse were the coins I had been saving to spend that day during the last hours of the Fair when all the bargains were to be had, and, even more important, the pass, signed by the Captain of the Ward, without which I might have difficulty in getting back into the city that night.

If I had known that that was the last time for many a long day that I was to leave my home without fear and walk boldly in daylight along the Close, I might have paused to look back at the fine house I was so proud of, though it had grown so shabby, and at the Castle, quiet above it, and the battery of guns like giant fingers spread menacingly over its roofs. I did not know: I did not look back. Whether my mother came to the window of the counting-house to see me go, as she often did, I could not tell, but I stiffened my back and held my head high defiantly—just in case.

Chapter 2

I passed through the water-gate on to the quayside. Without a glance to right or left, I threaded my way through the groups of sailors and merchants, keelmen, and idlers. Any other morning I would have paused and looked around to see if any of my friends were about. This morning, however, I did not want to meet anyone I knew; whether it was of pity, or scorn, or just curiosity, whatever look they met me with would hurt.

Fortunately, Jackie Armstrong was already on the quay looking out for me, so I would not have to hang about where everyone could see me. The keel—I noticed it was the *Emmet and Ralph*—was already full of coal, which must have been loaded at our staithes at Dent's Hole, a little farther down the river.

'What cheer, Master Ralph? What fettle the day, lad?' Jackie called out as soon as he saw me. 'Come on, jump in. You've slept in this morning, Ralph. Got out of the wrong side of the bed, an' all, by the looks of you. All right, shove off, lads: it's time for off.'

His voice was reassuringly normal. He could not yet have heard the news. I liked Jackie. He had worked for us for years, 'Since before you were born, Ralph lad,' as he was fond of telling me. Like many another keelman, he was a Borderer and had come from Elsdon in his youth. For some years he had gone back there each autumn when the coal trade came to a standstill on the river, and returned to Newcastle each spring when sailing began again. Then he had married one of my Grandfather Selby's maids and settled down in Sandgate and had seldom been back to his native heath since. His wife, like most native-born Tynesiders, had a wholesome fear of the borderlands and did not want her Jackie 'mixed up with them murdering mosstroopers any more'. If only half his tales of his wild kinfolk were true she did well to keep him away, although he always ended a tale with, 'Mind you, that was long ago; it's different now.'

Jackie himself always seemed such a mild man to have such lawless kin. He was little and thin, but very spry, and there was considerable strength in his wiry arms. He could handle either the swape of the keel, or the puy, and drive the vessel along as fast as any man on the Tyne, though now he was skipper of the keel he took a hand with the oars only occasionally. He had a lively face, with a network of good-humoured lines round his blue eyes and a very curious upper lip which looked as if two fingers had pressed the flesh below his nostrils so that his lips had, in compensation, pushed forward. I have since seen this characteristic in only one other person, and he was Jackie's brother.

At this moment Jackie was too busy with the keel to have time for much talk with me. He knew most of the watermen on the river and was hailed constantly from other keels as we made our way down the Tyne. From many of the colliers, too, a greeting was shouted to us across the water.

It was turning into a lovely day, and after a while I found it hard to stop myself from enjoying the fresh breeze and the steady progress of our keel through the tall-masted ships, and past the pleasant green meadows and trees on both banks of the river. The whole of this summer Emmet and I had been cooped up indoors by the prolonged wet, and inside the city walls by the regulations of the Governor and by my mother's fears.

'Well, hinnies,' said Jackie, with a look at the blue sky and soft clouds, 'this is one something they can't say they've prayed the Lord into.' The rest of the crew laughed. I came back into myself again. 'The weather, Ralph, the weather. It's looking up already, and they won't have started praying yet.' Then I remembered that this was to be a day of humiliation for more seasonable weather.

'They have, Jackie, an hour or more ago,' I said gloomily. 'They'll be sure they've won the Lord over, again.' All Parliament men believed that God was on their side, and not a few of the rest of us were beginning to wonder if they could be right.

So Jackie's joke was followed by a sober discussion. King's men that the men of this keel, like most of their fellows, were, they had to admit that things did not seem to be going well. Of course, it was difficult to know what was happening in other parts of the country, though fresh rumours had blazed along the quays and chares of Newcastle almost every day. The only information that we knew for certain to be true we would rather not have known: the Royalist forces in Northumberland had allowed themselves to be surprised near Eslington and Whittingham by Roundhead troops from Newcastle and the Bishopric under Colonel Wren, Colonel Fenwick, and Colonel Lilburne. The Royalists Colonel Grey and Colonel Tempest had been taken prisoner, and with them the Royalist gentry of Northumberland and Durham. Scarcely a blow had been struck: only the garrison of Cartington Castle had put up any resistance, and they had held out for only a few hours. My cousin, George Selby, had been captured there and was now imprisoned in Tynemouth Castle.

'No organization: we might as well admit it,' said Jem Allen.

'Mebbe,' said another of the crew, whose name I cannot remember. 'No money, more likely. Parliament's got the places where the money is—like Newcastle, for example.'

They all agreed with this. The remaining member of the crew, Tom Shafto, who was kept busy steering the keel by the swape at the back, and who had not joined in their discussion, reduced them all to silence with the gloomy remark that it didn't matter much to him who won. All he knew was that poor folks would get the rough end of the stick. 'We always do. Look at the price of bread now, and it's only August. What's it going to be before this winter's over?'

No one could find anything cheerful to say after this, not even Jackie. The wind dropped, and the sun grew warmer. It was hard work poling the keel downstream without any help from the sail, and no one spoke. But Jackie could not be melancholy for long.

'Well, me cannie lads, we've never died in winter yet,' he said. 'Though we've come bonnie and near it,' he added, with a grin, and began to whistle a tune. His cheerfulness was always as catching as the plague, and by the time we were sailing past Willington Quay we were all whistling or singing, and getting along in fine style to the accompaniment of the keelmen's own song, 'Weel may the keel row'.

At last we rounded a bend in the river and I could see in the distance a great column of smoke and steam so that I knew that we had nearly reached Shields.

As we passed the jetty at North Shields I could not help straining my eyes to see if Master Trumbell was about, though it was too early yet for our meeting. Of course, he was not: he was not a man to be either early or late.

The Cole salt-pans were between Shields and the river mouth, so we went past the little quay, past the new wagonway, almost as far as the Duke of Newcastle's fort at Low Light. Now I was too old for games, but the sight of the deserted fort, where Emmet and I had played Cavaliers and Scots only the previous summer, made me envious of my last year's self, and puzzled and angry that things could not go on always the same.

This summer had been so different from last. What would the next be like? I should be an apprentice then, and living at my master's house, unless—no, surely my mother could not change the old plan to apprentice me to Sir Francis Anderson, father of my friend Peter, and bind me instead to Thomas Trumbell, who was a hostman now. My indentures had not been signed yet, and now I came to think about it, no reference had been made to them of recent weeks. With a sinking heart I began to wonder if the plan had been changed. After all, if I were apprenticed to Trumbell, the question of a premium would not need to arise and I could still live at home. I began to feel sure my guess was right. Perhaps, I told myself frantically, if I went on refusing to speak to my mother and to Master Trumbell, they would keep to the original arrangements and let me go to Sir Francis. But how often had my mother allowed herself to be persuaded from her plans?

'Wake up, Ralph.' Jackie's voice brought me back with a jump. 'We're there.' He looked at me kindly.

'What's the matter, lad?' he asked. 'You've had a face like a motherless foal all the way down. Come on, out with it.'

His warm voice almost brought my tears to the surface, but though I had known him so long, and was very fond of him, I could not talk to anyone yet about my troubles and fears.

'Oh, leave me alone, will you?' I turned away from his hurt look, angry with myself and with him for being hurt, but not finding it in my heart to say I was sorry.

Jackie and his crew got straight on with their work of unloading the coals, while I made my way through the clouds of steam to find Will Reaveley, the overman. I peered into the first shed and called out to see if he was there. An old woman appeared through the smoke and steam and, in a surly voice, asked me what I was doing there. It was old Madge, whose work was to go round raking the dead ashes from under the

15

brine-pans. Her red-rimmed eyes peered at me, but, although she had seen me before, she did not recognize me. I asked where Will was.

'He's at the pump, trying to find out where the block is. The water's not coming through from the pit properly.' She turned to go back to her round of the pans. 'He's not in a very good skin about it, neither. So you'd better look out, lad,' she called over her shoulder.

I found Will bent over the pump, swearing at the pump-man and his marra.

'Ever since that fool went off for a soldier, there's been nowt but trouble with this thing,' he grumbled. 'He's the only man I've ever had who could keep it going. It's nearly worn out, anyway. We'll have to have a new one, I don't care what the Missus says. Oh——' he broke off. 'It's you, is it, Master Ralph? What do *you* want? You'll have to wait a minute. If I can't get the water through better than this I'll have to let some of the fires out, or the pans'll crack.'

'That's what I've come about,' I said, and I gave him my mother's message, with a certain amount of coldness, for he had not greeted me as his employer's son ought to be greeted.

Silence fell on the little group. My gaze left Will and passed to the other two men. The pump-man was looking full of fear and resentment: the other man pale, but resigned as if he were used to misfortune. I had been too busy with my own troubles to think what my message would mean to one of the men there. The looks on the faces staring at Will made me pause for a moment—but only for a moment. Another man was to be thrown on the scrap-heap of the workless. Ah, well, that was *his* problem, not ours. If there was no market for the salt we could not afford to go on making it.

Suddenly a succession of crumpled sounds startled us. It was almost funny the sudden way expressions changed and heads tilted to catch the sounds better. The sounds were repeated.

'Target practice,' I thought.

'I wonder what's up. Them's shots,' said one of the men. 'From a gun,' he added, with an air of surprise.

'Where'd you expect them to be from, you great daft gowk?' demanded Will Reaveley, glad of a chance to vent his worries on someone. 'Where's the guns, that's more to the point. Be quiet, the lot o' you, and listen.'

16

We waited: there was nothing but the startled screech of sea-gulls and the whirr of their wings.

Will Reaveley started muttering to himself: he seemed to have forgotten us. 'I don't like it. I don't like it at all. There's summat on up at the Castle. But what? That's what I'd like to know.'

His eye lighted on me. He roused himself with a visible effort.

'Now, Ralph,' he said, 'it's time you were off. I don't know what your mother's thinking of, letting you out of Newcastle at a time like this. Come on, let's see if them lazy beggars have finished unloading the coals. And you two,' he glared at the pump-man and the other workman, 'I'll be back in a minute. You heard the Missus's message. And you'd best have this pump fixed by the time I get back.'

He bustled me down the cinder path, through the clouds of vapour. He stopped and put his head through the doorway of the shed where old Madge was, and shouted to her not to put any more coals on the fires there. He was a good man for the Coles, I must admit, and never forgot our interests, which was why his rough freedom of speech was tolerated by us. But the other men did not like him: he was what they called 'a boss's man'.

By the time we reached the little jetty where the keel was, I was beginning to think Will was being officious, or maybe just anxious to get rid of me. The shots had not been repeated, so what could there be to worry about? Jackie and the other keel-men were busy unloading the coals exactly as usual and had not finished. Jackie looked up, surprised to see me back so soon: he knew I liked poking around the sheds, watching the brine going through the different stages between sea-water and black salt. Usually I had to be brought away from the salt-pans.

'My, you've been sharp,' he said. Then he must have noticed something unusual in our faces, or in mine at least: Will's was immutably fixed in lines of crabbiness. 'What's up?' he asked, looking from me to Will and back to me again.

'Didn't you hear the shots, Jackie?' I asked.

The men stopped unloading. Shots? No, they had heard nothing, but as Jackie said, 'When we're shovelling coals, Big Bess herself'—he was referring to Newcastle's biggest cannon—'could go off near wor ear-holes and we'd scarce notice, would we, lads?'

The men agreed. They were glad of the excuse to put down their shovels. But if they were prepared to spend the rest of the morning debating whether the shots meant that the Scots were at last attacking in Northumberland, or that the Prince of Wales had arrived just off the Tyne, or that any one of half a dozen things was happening, Will Reaveley was not prepared to let them. He started bustling the men to finish the unloading, thereby mortally offending Jackie, who told him to mind his own barrow and stick to his salt, and leave the keel to him. Angry words followed, but Will came off best in the end, because when Jackie eventually said the unloading was finished, Will accused him of leaving too much loose coal in the bottom of the keel, and refused to give him a tally for the coals until the men had swept up several more shovels of coal-dust.

While the dispute was going on I was hoping that they would not appeal to me, as the owner's son, for I liked Jackie and I did not like sour old Will Reaveley, who was, unfortunately, in the right, for it seemed to me that Jackie was indeed keeping back more than the recognized keelmen's sweepings. Learning to be a hostman was not going to be as easy as I had expected. However, it obviously never occurred to either of them to appeal to me. Perversely, I began to think that they should: after all, the disputed coals were, in a sense, mine. Yet I had not the courage to intervene: I could just imagine Will Reaveley telling me I was 'nowt but a bairn'. Since last night, nothing had seemed easy: misery settled on me once more and I just sulked in silence.

At last we got away, and set off upstream for the Shields jetty. The sun was by this time high in the sky and the keelmen decided that they might as well stay at Shields, when they had put me ashore, and have their bait there. They moored the keel and went off to the 'Salutation'. They said good-bye to me rather awkwardly, not quite liking to leave me on my own, yet not wanting the owner's son with them, though I don't suppose Jackie would have minded. Laughter and singing and the music of fiddlers bellied out as they pushed open the door of the inn and went inside. Jackie was the last and he turned round and waved to me. I hoped this meant he had forgiven me my surliness, and felt a little better.

There was nothing for it now but to go to meet Thomas Trumbell in the little shack at the end of the jetty which the

Newcastle guilds maintained as an office for their use when they were in North Shields, which was not seldom, for they guarded their monopolies zealously and kept a careful eye on the men of Shields who were inclined, quite unlawfully, to think themselves entitled to a share of the trade of the Tyne.

I refused to let my legs hurry me through the idlers on the quay to the office. I was surprised to find that my resentment of the factor had faded a little and to realize that there had actually been moments that morning when I had not even thought about him. Even hatred must rest at times, and after its rest it was, I was surprised to find out, not stronger but weaker.

By the time I was three-quarters of the way along the quayside, nervousness was my strongest feeling. What would Thomas Trumbell say to me? And what could I say to Thomas Trumbell? Overriding all was a silly, nagging anxiety about how to address him. As you can see, I was already wavering in my determination not to speak to him at all. I was beginning to realize that sooner or later I should have to address him, letting the thought sneak into my mind that it might be impossible to keep my morning vow of silence. But nothing, nothing, nothing, was going to make me behave agreeably towards him. Poor Thomas Trumbell! It never occurred to me that he might be anxious and embarrassed, too. Grown-ups never were. Why should they be?

I had almost reached the end of the quay. Shouting and a sudden clatter of hooves made me jerk round. Horsemen, scarlet-coated, except for one who seemed to lead them, had burst on to the quay. Whatever it was that the men were shouting, it flung the loungers into movement. The smooth stillness of the scene was gone and the whole quayside frothed with movement that threatened to submerge the horsemen.

I could see the excited gestures, I caught the note of urgency in the voices but not a word could I make out. I grabbed the arm of the man nearest me to ask him what had happened. He did not even notice me. But I had now moved near enough to see the facings of Colonel Henry Lilburne's regiment. Any boy growing up in Newcastle had had a chance to learn the facings of a number, first of Royalist regiments, then of Scottish regiments, and finally of Parliament regiments. Why, we used to 'collect' them, at school.

'What's up, Ralph?' asked a voice, and a hand grasped my elbow. It was Jackie.

'I don't know, Jackie,' I replied, 'but those are Henry Lilburne's men, I'm sure of it. They must be from the Castle. There's something going on there all right. Remember those shots Will Reaveley and I heard? D'you think some more prisoners have escaped?'

There was no time for Jackie to reply. The crowd was settling down to an excited quiet, and the horseman who appeared to be the leader was beginning to speak. I could hardly believe my eyes: he was someone I knew. He was my cousin, George Selby. But no, he could not possibly be. George Selby had been captured at Cartington Castle and was a prisoner in Tynemouth Castle. Then he must have escaped. But what could an escaped Royalist be doing in North Shields, in broad daylight, and in the company of officers of the regiment of the Roundhead Governor of Tynemouth Castle? It was mighty like George Selby all the same. I stared at him as hard as I could, so hard that for a moment or two only half my mind listened to what he was saying.

Jackie was still holding my elbow: he gripped it tightly as he listened, clearly not knowing what he was doing. He was grunting agreement with something the speaker was saying. The voice convinced me—it *was* George Selby. Then suddenly I realized, incredulously, what it was that my cousin was saying. Colonel Henry Lilburne, Deputy-Governor of Tynemouth Castle, had revolted from Parliament and was now holding the Castle for the King. We had almost grown accustomed to curious changes of side during recent months, but that a Lilburne should fight for King Charles seemed impossible. Yet, when I came to think of it, it was just like one of the crazy Lilburnes to turn over at the very moment when the King's party seemed to have ceased to be effective in Northumberland or Durham.

But I was giving my attention to George Selby now. He represented Lilburne's change of side as a practical man's solution to the state of deadlock the country had reached. We had a choice between King Charles and King Parliament. Lilburne had chosen the king appointed by God, not the many-headed, many-mouthed king, which was self-appointed. 'Choose the same way,' he shouted. 'If what we have now is freedom, give us back the old tyranny.' The crowd murmured agreement. He went on. Yes, Charles Stuart *had* made us pay illegal taxes. But what for? To build ships—to protect our own men and ships from pirates. 'You men of the Tyne, you know better than most that they were needed,' he said. *And* he'd taken the taxes from the folks that could spare them. King Parliament had taken more than any king ever had—and from everybody, poor as well as rich. As for breaking the law, what law gave Parliament the right to rob men—and their widows and orphans— for defending their anointed king? No honest man would give *that*—he clicked his fingers, and the crowd was so still that I heard the snap—for such a law.

'And what's happened,' he asked, 'to the lands, and money, and goods they've confiscated? It was to pay the soldiers, remember? And did it? There's many a lad was pressed to fight for them, and hasn't seen a brass farthing for months. And what about the men who were disbanded, and sent home with nothing but their wounds and bits of paper with worthless promises to pay them—some day? But have Hazelrigg and his sort gone short? Not he. He's getting richer every day. He'll own half the Tyne before he's finished—and his friends'll own the other half. And how many thousand will King Parliament vote him for his holy work of preserving the profits of the coal trade for himself and his friends?'

A voice shouted from the crowd—and we all craned our necks to try to see who was speaking. 'Shame on you, taking away the characters of honest men. Don't listen to him: you know the King's armies—sinners, every last man of them.'

But the crowd was not with him, and began to stir and mutter.

'Faith,' said George Selby, 'thou sayest true.' He paused dramatically. 'In our army we have the sins of men, drinking and wenching, but in yours you have those of devils, spiritual pride, and rebellion.'

The crowd roared its agreement, and George went on. One after another the accusations and dissatisfactions that for months, if not years, men had been muttering under their breaths were now shouted aloud for all to hear.

'And do you remember,' he asked, 'how they had plenty to say when the man, Charles Stuart,' he folded his hands and rolled his eyes piously to Heaven, a Presbyterian to the very life, and his audience roared in appreciation, 'tried to make us all conform to his Church—the Church, mind you, of Good Queen Bess.' Again, I could tell he had the crowd with him: by now, Elizabeth's reign had become a Golden Age. 'Oh, aye,' said he, 'they had plenty to say then, but when *they* force *their* church on us, that's all right. That's fine. It's the Church of England folk, not only the Papists, that must meet in hiding-places now. And what's more, they can't even agree what their own church is. Are they Presbyterians or Independents? Are they going to *dig* or *level*, or what?'

If there were any Independents, Presbyterians, Diggers, or Levellers in that crowd, they had wit enough to keep quiet. By now the majority of us were feathers for George Selby to blow which way he pleased.

'King Parliament,' he cried, 'has grown too great. Men who fight for their lawful king are now being called rebels—rebels against King Parliament—and are being found guilty of treason. What kind of double-talk is this, tell me that. Their words don't make sense any more. They keep the King shut up in prison and say they are "protecting" him. Who are they protecting him from? They're the only ones who wish him any harm. We all know that the Parliament men are plotting to kill him.' A gasp went through the crowd. 'Oh, yes, they are. And don't go on saying, "They'd never dare," until it's been done.'

Kill the King? Surely George Selby was going too far, now. Kings had been killed by their subjects before, but they had been wicked men. No one had ever been able to call King Charles a wicked man—not so that anyone really believed it. But I was missing some of George Selby's words.

'. . . in Newcastle, when he was a prisoner of the Scots, before they sold him to Parliament. Oh, aye, these lovers of liberty buy and sell men. How many free-born Englishmen have they sold like cattle to be shipped to die as slaves in the plantations of America and the Indies, or over the oars of the galleys of the Venetians? You are all free-born Englishmen. Are you going to stand idle and let them do that to other free men?

'The name of Lilburne means something in these parts—nay, not only in these parts but in the whole of England. Colonel Henry Lilburne, own brother to Honest John—you know Honest John. Who doesn't?' A murmur of agreement rippled through the crowd. 'And just like him,' he went on, 'afraid of nothing and nobody when freedom's at stake. He's shown you the way. Come with me and join him and his men and show King Parliament that the cannie lads of the Tyne are not afraid of it—or its New Noddle Army.'

We laughed as if it were the first time we had ever heard that name, and the terrible New Model Army dwindled, for a few crazy minutes, into a joke.

'Now, who's for King Charles?' shouted George Selby, and a tremendous yell answered him. Somewhere in it I heard my own voice. I suddenly realized that the muscles of my face and neck were tight with the intensity of my listening, and it was a relief to scream with the crowd. Jackie Armstrong, still at my elbow, snatched off his bonnet and threw it into the air like a schoolboy.

George Selby was turning his horse back in the direction from which he had come. He drew his sword and brandished it, and he seemed to me like one of the knights of old.

'Follow me!' he cried, and, so sure of us was he now, he turned his back on us and urged his horse forward. There was a second's pause and then a surge to follow him. Jackie was one of the first to move: his reactions were always quick. Just in front of me a woman was clinging to the arm of a giant of a man, crying and holding him back. Like a bear in the pit with its first attacker, he flung her off, so roughly that she stumbled and almost fell. 'That's right,' I thought, 'that's the way to treat her.' Women always wanted to play safe. I had had enough of being ruled by women. At last I had a chance to show that I was a man now, not a child to be ordered about any longer. I would choose my own side, and not be dragged along behind a woman's skirts, to be kept safe no matter what happened: safe, if Parliament were victorious, because Thomas Trumbell was a friend of Parliament men; safe, if the King came into his own again, because my name was Cole, because my grandfather had been Sir George Selby; above all, because my father had died for him at the siege of Newcastle. Safe, safe, safe. Who, at fifteen, thinks that he wants to be safe? So I was one of the ill-fated mob that streamed after George Selby on that bright August day in 1648.

By what strange freak of sound I heard it, I do not know, but out of the babel on the quay at that moment, I suddenly heard a voice.

'Ralph, Ralph, come back, lad. Come back. Don't be a fool.

They haven't a chance. Wait a minute, wait for me.'

It was Thomas Trumbell. I did not turn round. I pushed deeper into the crowd. I had just escaped in time.

Chapter 3

When we came near the Castle, George Selby galloped off ahead of us, so that by the time we reached it the gate was already open and the drawbridge down in readiness for us. We had been half-walking, half-running, in a loose, spread-out column. As we funnelled into the narrow barbican, we came together in a tight throng. Some of my feeling of exaltation left me. An unreasonable and unreasoning fear of being suffocated, which always comes on me when I am shut in a narrow, crowded space, beat in my throat. Then the man behind me, who was pressing me forward, trod heavily on the back of my shoe so that it no longer gripped my foot, and I stepped out of it. It was impossible to bend down in that mob (for that moment it was a mob to me, not a band of fellow volunteers) to pick it up. I was forced on. There were three gateways to pass through; by the time I was through the last one, my foot was sore and bruised.

. The others fanned out into the courtyard beyond the Gatehouse, but I stopped and waited for the moment when I could go back for my shoe.

The torrent of volunteers soon became a trickle. They were not, I noticed with my first misgivings, nearly as many as I had thought. As I stood hesitating, about to plunge back through the gateway, I was startled by a hand laid on my arm and a voice which hissed in my ear, 'Don't stand there with that look on your face for everybody to see what you're thinking, you young fool,' and I was pulled back from the gateway with such a jerk that I lost my balance and almost fell. It was Jackie. I stared at him in amazement. I suddenly realized that I had never seen him really angry before, but there was no mistaking his mood now. The invisible fingers were pressing harder than usual and leaving frightening white marks round his nostrils, and dragging the laughter wrinkles out of their old pleasant pattern into new shapes of anger.

'You young fool,' he repeated. 'What did you have to come here for? This is none of *your* business. Hasn't your mother had trouble enough, without this? You've rushed into this like a mad bull, and already you're wanting to rush out of it.'

I could feel the smile of pleasure and relief that my first recognition of him had brought to my lips stiffen on my face. I was utterly taken aback both by his savage tone, so unfamiliar, and by his complete misunderstanding of my feelings and intentions at that moment. 'But Jackie . . .' I tried to explain, but he shook off my words.

'Haven't you sense enough to realize that nobody's going to get out of here today, or for many a long day after, neither? There's been one man run through already this day for wanting to get out. Aye, run through by his own colonel, Lilburne, that he'd served under since the beginning of the first war.' Jackie had evidently been keeping his ears open in the few minutes he had been in Tynemouth Castle. I found time to think this, even as he was speaking—and to begin to realize that it was something more than a schoolboy's game I had embarked on this time. He was going on as if I had raised an objection to what he had just said: 'Oh, yes, a few got away— they'll be nearly to Newcastle by now, to fetch Hazelrigg down against us—but *they* had muskets. And *they* didn't get out through those gates. Oh no, *they* got over the wall.'

I found myself looking up at the grim walls above me, and thinking of the cruel drop at the other side.

'There'll be nobody else'll get out of here,' said Jackie. 'Lilburne'll see to that. Do you realize that he can't be sure of a single man among us? Any one of us could be a spy for Parliament. Why: I might be. So might you. You'll not get away to tell tales to Hazelrigg. Now d'you see what a mess you've got yourself into?'

I could, only too well.

'And you'll have to fend for yourself,' Jackie was going on. 'I didn't come here to be a nursemaid to you, I can tell you.'

I could have burst into tears at hearing such words from my kind-hearted friend. Then he looked at me and must have seen my surprise and hurt, and his tone softened.

'Well, lad, it's no good standing there, with a look like a motherless foal,' said he, and he took refuge in proverb: 'What can't be cured must be endured. Never mind what I said the now, Ralph hinnie: you stick with me, and maybe we'll come out of this better than the pair of us deserve.'

At last he was willing to listen to me, so I was able to explain that all I had wanted was to go back to the barbican to find my shoe. He stared at me in surprise and then glanced down at my shoeless foot, and, unexpectedly, burst into a great roar of laughter. After a moment's indignation, I found myself joining in, and we laughed and laughed until the tears came. I was suddenly sobered by a not too gentle push in the ribs from a musket which belonged to an indignant and suspicious sergeant of Lilburne's regiment. I became aware, to my embarrassment, that everyone had grown quiet and that we were being watched by many curious eyes. The sergeant gestured to us to go and join the main body of recruits who now formed a group—not a very big one—in the middle of the Great Court, while members of the original garrison, easily distinguishable by their scarlet uniforms, were spaced round the edges of the court. I would have gone without a word, but Jackie said calmly, 'The lad's lost a shoe back there; just hold on a minute while I fetch it.' And he darted off and was back with it, almost

27

before the gaping sergeant had closed his mouth again.

Jackie moved forward first and I hobbled after him, not daring to stop to put on that confounded shoe, now sadly trampled out of shape. Just as we took our places with the other recruits a small group of officers, headed by a tall, grim-faced man in a scarlet uniform with sash and collar of silver lace, appeared at the end of the court. The soldiers stiffened even more woodenly. I found myself straightening my back and shoulders. We knew without being told that this was Lieutenant-Colonel Henry Lilburne.

An untidy cheer began to waver through the crowd, but he raised his hand for silence and began to speak. He briefly welcomed us in the name of the King. Then he told us that throughout the country fortresses were declaring against Parliament. A brief hope flashed through my mind, and I waited for him to say that Newcastle itself was turning over on this very same day. But no: he was going on to tell us that we had a more important part to play than most. If we held out at Tynemouth, we could influence the whole course of the new war, for Tynemouth Castle, he said, commanded the mouth of the Tyne and could prevent ships entering or leaving the Tyne, and so bring the coal trade to a standstill.

'London can't do without Newcastle coal,' he said. 'Parliament found that out four years ago. Londoners are hesitating—aye, even Londoners are beginning to sicken of their new masters. A winter without coal will make up their minds for them. So it's up to us, men, to see that that's what they get. We must hold on here. And there's no reason why we shouldn't. This garrison is well-provisioned, well-armed, and,' he allowed himself a grim smile, 'well-manned.' The men raised a good-humoured cheer in acknowledgement of this.

He concluded by saying that there was no time to be wasted as we must be ready to stand a siege or a storm at any moment, so the Articles of War would be read to us and the oath administered to us all together, immediately afterwards. Then we were to be organized for the work we could most usefully do. He handed us over to his senior officer and himself withdrew.

It was not very easy to hear every word of the Articles. The wind was blowing in gusts from the sea—which I had not seen yet, although the castle stood on a headland—and played tricks, sometimes seeming to magnify the speaker's voice, at other

28

moments roaring in my ears and drowning the words I was trying to hear. In addition, there was a deal of noise around us as the old members of the garrison went about their business of last minute preparations for the siege that was almost certainly imminent. The voice was reading the Ordinances of War, the rules by which I should have to live from now on. I had never realized that there were so many. As the voice went on and on endlessly, I began to feel alarmed: I could never remember all these regulations. Why, boys at school had not so many; nor even apprentices in the Hostmen's Guild. And the punishment for breaking these rules was not a birching, but something worse, much worse.

'He that absents himself when the sign is given to set the Watch shall be punished at discretion, either with Bread and Water in Prison or with the Wooden Horse.

'No man shall depart a mile out of the Army or Camp without licence, upon pain of death.

'No man shall give a false Alarum or discharge a Piece in the night, or make any noise without lawful cause, upon pain of death.'

The castle gates behind us crashed open. My attention wandered as a few bewildered cows were driven past us by a party of returned foragers. The voice had not paused, however.

'. . . upon pain of death.'

I hastened to reassure myself that I could find out from Jackie what I had missed and set myself to listen again.

'Whosoever shall express his discontent with the Quarter given him in the Camp, or Garrison, shall be punished as a Mutineer.

'No person shall make any mutinous assemblies or be present or assisting thereto, or in, or by them demand their pay, upon pain of death.'

Death. Death again. For demanding one's pay.

Item after item was read out. I was finding it hard to concentrate now. A cock crowed triumphantly from the barnyard; the sound was strangely peaceful: what had it to do with the world into which I had just thrust myself? The ordinariness of it did nothing to lessen my rising panic, but, rather, increased it, for I had no place in a safe, ordinary world any more. I could hear the officer's voice quite well now, yet my brain did not make sense of any of the words, except the terrible ones with which each and all of the Ordinances now seemed to be ending.

'. . . upon pain of death.

'. . . upon pain of death.

'. . . shall be punished with DEATH.'

And now I really did want to turn and run home. I could never remember all these rules: I was bound to break one, unwittingly. I knew the rigid discipline that officers of the New Model Army—and Lilburne had been one of them until this morning—were accustomed to enforce. I recalled the dangling bodies of soldiers left hanging on the gallows in Newcastle for days as a warning to their comrades and a declaration to the town that the forces of Parliament stood for law and order. In the few minutes I stood there, I began to realize what it was like to be unprotected by rank, or money, or privilege. Most of the men around me had belonged to the unprotected all their lives—I could see that just by looking at the clothes they wore. Yet, strangely, my panic began to subside as I looked at them. Far from being frightened, they appeared, rather, quite uninterested in the relentless voice that still went on and on. The man in front of me scratched his grimy neck in boredom, and moved restlessly from foot to foot. Little shuffling sounds were spreading through the whole group. No one else seemed unduly alarmed. I took heart. What use was I going to be to King Charles or Colonel Lilburne or even to myself if, before a blow was struck, I was scared by the thought of the rules of my own side.

I have known, since that day, many a man who has said that he suffers his worst doubts and fears before he makes a decision of importance. That has never been my way. Some force which almost seems to be outside myself pushes me into taking a course of action, not only without hesitation but even with exhilaration; pushes me so far that I cannot draw back. Then, treacherously, the impetus leaves me to the anxieties and doubts which, too late, come crowding in upon me. This is something I noticed for the first time on the day I am talking about. This was the first time I had experienced such an unpleasant seesawing of feelings, because never before had I, entirely on my own, taken an irrevocable step—one which, only too clearly, was going to affect the course, not only of my own life but, conceivably, the life of others. For the first time since leaving the quay at North Shields I thought of my mother and of Emmet, wise Emmet who always did as she was told, and wondered how they would feel when Thomas Trumbell told them what I had done. Now that I might never see them again, I wished that I had not left home in such an ugly mood and without even saying good-bye. And all because my mother was going to marry Thomas Trumbell and I was ashamed to call him stepfather. With a sickening feeling of doubt, at last I allowed myself to look at the possibility that my fine gesture in following George Selby to Tynemouth Castle might have been made, not out of loyalty to King Charles, but out of a wish to run away from what my friends might be thinking and saying about Thomas Trumbell. But I soon pushed the thought away. I was a Royalist by birth and by inclination. I had more reason for following the King than most of the poor, half-starved souls around me.

My mother's father, Sir George Selby, had counted it a privilege to spend a fortune which he could well afford entertaining King James in Newcastle, and, until the day of his death, had gloried in his nickname, 'the King's Host'. My father had given his life for King Charles. And had he not always taught me to believe that my own fate was specially linked to King Charles? He had never tired of telling me that the day when I was born, 3 June 1633, was the day when King Charles, on his way to his coronation in his Scottish Kingdom, had entered Newcastle for the first time. My uncle, my father's brother, Ralph Cole (whose namesake I am) was Mayor of the city that year, and it was at his house that King Charles stayed. It had seemed a good omen to the Coles that the newest member of the family should make his appearance in the world at the very moment that the bells pealed and the guns were fired to tell the citizens that King Charles had set foot on Newcastle bridge. At the banquet given for the King that evening, my uncle, the Mayor, made bold perhaps by the wine he had drunk, told the tale to the King. Now, strange though it may seem, no one knew better than Charles Stuart how to make men love him: his enemies were those who knew him least. He asked that my father should be presented to him, spoke to him, though what he said my father was too overcome to remember very accurately, and then called on all the guests to drink the health of, as he put it, the young man who had entered Newcastle for the first time at the same moment as himself. Then he drew from his finger a ring which he gave to my father as a birth gift

31

for me. Yes, it is this same ring which I am wearing today. Thus easily he made my father, and indeed me also, his man for the rest of his life.

All these thoughts went through my head far more quickly than it takes me to tell you them—and far less smoothly. But of all the threads tangled in the ravelled skein of my thoughts and feelings on that day long ago, the brightest was the memory that my father had fought and died for King Charles and it could not, therefore, be wrong for me to join in the same fight. So now, in that crowded courtyard, slowly returning to awareness of the steady drone of the officer's voice, still, to my surprise, intoning the Ordinances of War, though I was bewildered by the realization for the first time in my life of the complexity of my own motives, I was also heartened by a conviction that I had had more solid reasons for my sudden action than, a few moments before, I had feared.

Then it occurred to me that Jackie also must have been going through the same extremes of exaltation and panic as I had: that would account for the departure from his usual calm good humour that had so startled me a few minutes ago. It had never even crossed my mind before that grown-ups also could suffer doubts and uncertainties. The gap between myself and them was suddenly very narrow.

The officer's voice stopped at last. Then another voice called, 'God save the King,' and in a second we were released from our trance and were shouting our throats out.

We all took the oath together and then we were handed over to the sergeant, who marched us off, in ragged order, to the armoury, to sign the muster roll, to be issued with our weapons and then assigned to our officers. Here again we found ourselves waiting. The whole fortress was feverish with preparation, excitement, and anticipation, yet I seemed to be doing nothing that afternoon but stand about in idleness. My stomach might be knotted with impatience, but I had to take my place in the queue that was slowly moving forward into the shell of the older church, where a table had been set up in the ruined choir. There an officer was taking men's names and adding them to the muster roll.

Jackie and I stayed together but neither of us was finding anything to say just then. As we drew near the table we found that a second officer was asking each man about his experience of fighting and of weapons and assigning him to a troop accordingly. Jackie turned to me and said, in a low voice, 'I used a musket at the Newcastle siege, Ralph. If we want to keep together, that'd better be the thing you can do as well.'

'But, Jackie, I've never fired one in my life. They'd soon find that out.'

'By that time they'll have their companies made up and won't want to change them. Anyway, the first spare minute we get, I'll show you how. A sharp lad like you'll get the knack of it in next to no time.'

With some misgivings, I agreed. I wanted to stay with Jackie, but the memory of the cruel penalties listed in the Articles of War for so many offences—perhaps lying was one of them— was still nagging at the back of my mind.

At last it was Jackie's turn. He gave his name, watched the officer enter it on the muster roll, made his mark opposite it, and passed to the next officer.

Now I stepped forward. The muster officer reeled off a warning against giving a false answer, and asked my name. There was no flicker of recognition from him when I said, 'Ralph Cole, sir,' which chagrined me a little, for other bearers of it, my kin, had made it a name well-known along the Tyne. He did show a gleam of surprise when he saw that I could write my name, but he passed me on to his companion without comment.

'Ever served before—either side?'

'No, sir.'

'Been in a trained band?'

'No, sir.'

'Ever used a musket, firelock, pistol, or sword?'

I had fully intended to say that I had used a musket, and yet I heard myself say, without an instant's conscious thought, 'No, sir.'

'Captain Selby's troop for you, then.'

This was a stroke of luck I had scarcely hoped for: it made up, a little, for being separated from Jackie. I hurried after him and, as we entered the armoury together, I told him what had happened. He smiled with something like a flash of his old good humour.

'Nay, lad, Ralph,' he said slyly, 'they'll never make a host-man out of you: you're too honest for your own good.'

I did not know whether to laugh or be indignant. Before I

could make up my mind we had to separate, for Jackie was directed to one end of the armoury and I was sent to the other.

Again there was a queue and a wait. I scarcely noticed my fellow soldiers at first for my attention was taken immediately by the pile of weapons stacked beside a perspiring corporal, who was issuing them while a sergeant kept a record of the issue. I could not believe my eyes: the weapon being given to each man to defend himself, the Castle, and the cause of the King, was—a scythe. There was muttering among the men. They were clearly as dismayed as I was. I wished I had not been so truthful; probably they did, too. Nobody durst murmur openly, however: the sergeant was still wearing the uniform of the New Model Army. It was a dejected group that made its way out of the armoury.

I tried to chase the foreboding from my bones by looking at the men who were likely to be my companions for some time to come. The man who had happened to be behind me in the queue in the armoury was strange enough to attract attention at any time. He was a large man and the largest thing about him was his pale, bald head, fringed by a few tassels of black hair. His neck and his face where it was not bristling with some days' blue-black growth of beard were deeply tanned like a countryman's. The contrast between his weathered face and his pale, cloistered head was startling, and I never did find out the reason for it. No, it could not have been that he normally wore a wig: this was before men took to wearing wigs. He had with him a sad little mongrel that seemed afraid to be farther than a few inches away from its master.

No one in our group quite liked to be the one to start talking so the dog came in for a lot of patting and scratching, but it remained unmoved: it was strange the way it ignored the overtures of the men, neither accepting nor rejecting them. Its owner remained expressionless also: he did not seem to notice either his dog or the men trying to make friends with it, and soon we all subsided into an uneasy and resentful silence. The big man with the pale head was the most conspicuous figure in the troop I had been assigned to. I decided to keep my eyes on him: he would be easy to keep in sight. Since Jackie had disappeared I was terrified of getting separated from my troop and of having to ask questions of strangers. Very shortly, however, the last of our troop came from the armoury and was followed not long afterwards by the corporal who had been giving out the weapons.

He took charge of us and marched us to another part of the fortress. In an upstairs room we waited in yet another queue while the day's rations were weighed out for us. Then in an adjacent building—another queue—we were issued with canvas knapsacks in which to keep our rations. There were not enough uniforms to supply us all: what there were had gone to the musketeers, we discovered. There was grumbling about this. I was beginning to suspect that some of the recruits had joined the garrison for the sake of the rations of food and clothing they expected to get. For myself, I did not mind the lack of uniform—the only ones in the garrison were Parliament's and I had no wish to wear the same uniform as the King's enemies.

At last we were led to our quarters, a long wooden hut, one of a number which had been erected among the ruins of the old Priory cloister. The corporal left us with a warning that we had not much time to settle ourselves in and have something to eat before he came back to give us our duties for the next twenty-four hours.

I hung back while the others established themselves in the hut and it was the pallet in the draughty place opposite the door that was left for me. I sat down on it and made myself busy with my rations to cover my shyness. Besides, I was hungry. I spread out my portion: two bottles of beer, two pounds of bread, one pound of cheese; poor enough fare, it seemed to me, and not much for twenty-four hours. I should have eaten more of the bread and cheese Alyse had set before me that morning. Surely it could not have been only that morning? It seemed a lifetime away. And last night's supper I had gone without, too. There had probably been capon, and fresh fish, and red meat, and white bread; and almonds and raisins and ginger after the custard coffins; for my uncle from Antwerp was in the house, and my mother would have been ashamed not to offer a guest a sufficient meal, even in these hard times. Then I remembered the food Alyse had given me: I would keep it until I really needed it; neat's tongue might be a treat in the days to come. I was learning fast. I hacked off a piece of the coarse barley bread with my knife. Then I sawed at the lump of cheese, which was so hard I could scarcely get my knife through it, and began my meal.

The men's first awkwardness was past now. They all—all, that is, except the big man and me—were talking fast and loudly: each seemed to be trying to establish his position in the group. They talked mostly about how well Tynemouth must be provisioned for a siege. It was widely known that Parliament had laid up in all its fortresses enough meat and drink to last six months. This they believed, but all the same each man found it necessary to say it aloud for himself, I noticed.

'Good job for you, old lad,' said a little man whose grey complexion proclaimed him a miner. He scratched the unresponsive ear of the mongrel that still sat at the big man's heels. 'You might be wor Christmas dinner, else.' He laughed in huge delight at his own joke, throwing back his head and showing a mouth full of broken teeth. The others joined in, one or two not quite so whole-heartedly. The owner of the dog turned his expressionless gaze on them and the laughter died out uneasily.

The little miner was not to be subdued for long.

'Looks as if we might be marras for a cannie while,' he said. 'Suppose we find out who we all are. I'm Zouch Tate of Chilton, pitman, or I was until the pit was drowned last May. Since then I've been owt or nowt, mostly nowt and bonnie and hungry an' all.' He turned suddenly to me. 'What's your name, hinnie?'

'Ralph.' I was startled.

'Ralph what?'

'Ralph Cole.'

They all stared at me.

'That's not a good name in these parts,' said the pitman. 'Any relation to the old skinflint in Newcastle who goes by that name?'

I was so surprised to hear genial Uncle Ralph described like this that I did not answer at once.

'Nay, I can see you're not.' He made a comical bow to me. 'Humble apologies. There's plenty of *honest* folk by the name of Cole, and none of them'd be hostmen.'

He turned his attention to another man who said he was from Tynemouth. My Uncle Ralph a skinflint! I could hardly believe my ears. Why, he was one of the most generous men alive. And what had—what was his name?—Zouch Tate meant by saying that there were plenty of *honest* folk by the name of Cole? I knew that there were envious men, both inside and outside Newcastle, who attacked the powers of the Host-men's Guild, of all the guilds for that matter, but I had been brought up to believe that only the hostmen knew how to run the coal trade on which the Tyne depended. Even Parliament had had to admit that. And I had heard often enough that every man on the Tyne should be grateful to the hostmen who put the bread in his mouth. But here was one who showed no signs of gratitude at all. I had already noticed his poor clothes and thin face, and a doubt was sown in my mind that perhaps he had not a great deal to be grateful for. For the moment I put the thought out of reach—I had had enough new ex-periences to deal with for one day.

While I had been struggling with these new thoughts, I had missed the names and self-descriptions of most of my fellow soldiers. There was, it appeared, only the big man with the dog left. There was a second's hesitation on the part of Zouch Tate, but only a second's.

'Well, mate,' he said, 'what about you?'

All eyes were fixed on the big man. I think we expected him to refuse to answer. But no, expressionless as ever, he replied, 'Ambrose Grimston,' and then after a slight pause, 'of Ogle.'

Not a soul in Newcastle did not know that the core of the Duke of Newcastle's White Coats, in the First War, had come from Ogle and the neighbouring parts of Northumberland. And there was not a soul in the whole of England who did not know how the White Coats had fought and died for the King at Marston Moor; or how dearly they had fulfilled their pledge that their white coats would be made scarlet. But it was their own blood, not their foes', that had dyed those coats. The men in that hut had been ready enough earlier to exchange crumbs of battle gossip, but there was not a man among them, not even sparrow-bold Zouch Tate, who durst ask Ambrose Grimston a single question about Marston Moor.

An uneasy moment went by, then two or three different conversations began in the hut. I felt miserable because there was no group to which I seemed to belong and I did not want to be left alone with my thoughts. Fortunately, a few moments later there was noise outside, then a great thumping at the door, which next instant opened, crashing against the bottom of my pallet, so that I realized why that particular one had been left to me: it was the corporal.

'Come on, lads, now. There's plenty of work to be done. Look sharp, there.'

The break was over: it was time to begin being a soldier at last.

Chapter 4

I scrambled quickly to my feet, pleased at the prospect of having something definite to do. I do not know what I expected a soldier's duties to be: most likely something romantic such as patrolling the Castle, sword in hand (though we had no swords), and scanning the horizon for the first sight of the Roundheads and I, of course, would be the one to give the alarm; or even, just learning to load and fire a musket; or, at the very worst, drilling in formations in the courtyard. In fact I became one of a small group sent to the unmilitary task of looking after the cattle and poultry. The corporal had left us, after telling us how to get to the poultry-yard.

'Sent to feed the bloomin' hens,' said the Tynemouth man, 'and Hazelrigg and his Lobsters due any minute.'

To get to the poultry-yard, which was on the north side of the promontory on which the Castle stood, we had to go through the Inner Court, then through the Great Court. The Inner Court was comparatively quiet. Musketeers were going through all the steps of practising the loading of their muskets. I caught sight of Jackie among them. He saw me, too, and his face gave a comical twist of recognition which was all he could manage, I guessed, without swallowing the bullets he had in his mouth. At the opposite side of the court another small group was drilling with pikes.

We left the Inner Court and came to the Great Court and a scene much more like a market-place than a fortress, for here requisitioning parties were bringing their spoils: hay, coals, faggots, animals. We found ourselves leaping out of the path of a flock of frightened sheep that swirled around our legs like muddy water and threatened to submerge us.

'Let's be out of this, lads,' cried Zouch Tate, and he marshalled us off to the barnyard. Even this was a scene of stir, where disturbed hens fled, squawking indignantly, from the strangers among them, cocks stretched their necks at new rivals, and disorientated ducks waddled disconsolately after a forlorn leader, looking, without much hope, for the old familiar pond.

It was hard work feeding and settling down first these agitated fowls, and afterwards, the terrified beasts which had been snatched, an hour or two before, by rough hands, from safe familiar surroundings. The most useful man among us was Ambrose Grimston, the big man from Ogle. He seemed to be used to handling animals and besides he was so strong that he could carry a struggling pig under each arm and, at the same time, with his hip give a stubborn cow or bullock a push which left it in no doubt about the way it must go. He worked without a word. And all the time the mongrel clung to his heels, miraculously avoiding the feet and hooves around him.

The late afternoon sun was hot and the breeze had dropped while we were working. Even when twilight came, the air stayed warm and still and we were glad when the last beast had been fed and watered and bestowed in its place and our corporal, who had rejoined us and been working with us for some time, said we might rest where we were for a few minutes while he found out what our next orders were.

We were too tired to have much to say as we rested. It was easy to see that Zouch had been a collier: he sat on his hunkers with hands resting on his thighs, while the rest of us sat with our backs against the old stone walls of the Great Barn, still warm from the sun.

After an interval of time which I had no way of measuring (never before had I been so long out of the sight of St. Nicholas's friendly face), our corporal returned and gave us our orders for the night. We were to sleep for the first part of the night and then stand watch until sunrise, when we were to be relieved. It appeared that Colonel Lilburne was fairly confident that Hazelrigg could not get an attacking force into position before the next morning, and he wanted to keep his experienced troops fresh until then. If, by some miracle, Hazelrigg did get his men to Tynemouth during the night, it was hardly likely that he would try to storm the Castle before daylight. Anyway a siege was much more likely, said the corporal wisely. Nevertheless, just in case, we were to be stiffened by the addition of some of Lilburne's own men. And the cannon would be manned and at the ready. Then our corporal—I never did learn the man's name—gave us the field word for the night, marched us back to our quarters and dismissed us to sleep, if we could, until it was time to stand our watch.

I had a silly fear that I might forget the field word, though

Heaven knew, it could scarcely have been easier—'God and the King'. I was still mouthing it under my breath, like a zany, as I stretched out on my hard pallet. Then, suddenly it lost all meaning and became a senseless jumble of sounds, and in fright I stopped and tried to get some sleep. Too much had happened that day: round and round my brain raced thoughts of Alyse and Emmet, of my mother and Thomas Trumbell, even of old Will Reaveley and the man to be dismissed that morning, and, of course, of Jackie. When should I see any of them again, even Jackie? As I tossed and turned, the subdued murmurs of the men gradually died down and only I seemed to be left awake. I half raised myself on my elbow to see if anyone else *was* awake, and there was the big man, on his knees and muttering to himself. Then he made the sign of the cross: the man was praying. A moment later, in the twilight of that summer night, I saw that he held in his hands a string of beads. There was such rapt concentration in every line of him that I lowered myself gently back on to my pallet in order not to disturb him. How strange that a great giant of a man like him should be playing with a string of beads, I thought, muddled with the need to sleep. Then I realized what it must be. Not that I had ever seen a rosary—all my life, careful folk kept such things out of sight; a man might die merely for possessing one.

Merciful Heavens, the man was a Papist.

Chapter 5

My discovery made me feel less like sleep than ever. Alyse—
and not only Alyse—had filled us since babyhood with stories
of Papists, their secret rites and their human sacrifices. She
relished the punishments meted out to them: fines, confiscation
of property, the pillory, the rack, and death in its most hideous
form. She had made them seem a different race from ordinary
folk. I scarcely know which made them seem more frightening
to me—the unknown things they did at their secret ceremonies,
or the known horrors of their sufferings when they were
discovered. The big man, already a frightening figure with his
huge body and huge strength and huge quietness, seemed no
different from a warlock chanting spells or prayers to his master
the Auld Lad, the Devil himself. I felt lonelier at that moment
than I had ever felt in my life before. I was filled with an over-
whelming longing for my own bed at home in the Close. That
was where I should be, peacefully asleep, surrounded by folks
I had known all my life. Then I remembered the two Parliament men billeted with us. Of course, Harbottle Grimston.
Grimston. That was the big man's name. The name had been
tantalizing me at odd moments since he had given it. Ambrose
Grimston. Harbottle Grimston. Harbottle Grimston was
Captain Simpson's Lieutenant. I had last seen him—could it
possibly be only that morning? I tried to remember what he
looked like; but then I had always avoided looking directly at
him, and I had kept out of his way as much as possible. If I
had looked at him it had been his hated uniform I had seen.
Could he be kin to the man praying over there? He also was an
unusually big man, and Grimston was not a very common
name. But a practising Catholic and a preaching Presbyterian
kin? Impossible, surely. Yet the possibility remained—families
were divided—and joined the dreary circle chasing round my
brain.

How much longer I tossed on my uncomfortable pallet I do
not know, but I scarcely seemed to have closed my eyes at
last, when I was being shaken awake to take my turn at standing watch with the rest of the troop. Someone had lit a rush-

light and I could see the corporal and Zouch Tate and the others already eating a meal of bread and cheese. I tried to follow their example but the bread stuck in my mouth and though I chewed and chewed I did not seem able to swallow it. I stuffed some of my rations into my pocket, hoping that I might get a chance to eat later on if I felt hungry. As yet I had no idea what would be expected of me. I had seen men on watch on the walls of Newcastle, but for the last four years they had been such a commonplace of existence that I had never really noticed what they did. In fact, I was beginning to realize that there were a lot of things I had seen without noticing them.

We were placed on the stretch of wall between the Gatehouse and the Whitley Tower. It was dark as we exchanged in whispers the field sign with the men we were relieving. Inside the walls an occasional flicker of light showed that others besides ourselves were awake and busy, but beyond the walls there was not a glimmer anywhere. The silence was almost as complete. Once or twice I heard the ring of metal, but that was all. I settled down to the task of watching, listening. Only a few feet away on one side of me was a musketeer and a few feet on the other Grimston, and others beyond them, but in the darkness and stillness I might have been alone in a newly-made world, with the only reality the sound of my own breathing. Once I bumped my scythe against the wall and the startled curse from the musketeer showed that I was not the only one there whose nerves were strained to the edge of endurance.

Little by little I sensed a relaxation of tension along the wall. A man cleared his throat; another blew on his fingers—it was cold up here in the night breeze. After all, no one seriously expected anything to happen before morning. Anyway—best thought of all—was there not every hope that the Royalists had taken over Newcastle also? I stifled the thought that if they had we could have heard by now: after all, there would have been fighting; Newcastle was a city, not a single fortress like Tynemouth. There must have been some reason (or so I thought) why Lilburne had declared for the King on this particular day. There must be some wider plan. Perhaps the Scots had at last come to the aid of the King: they seemed to be just as ready to fight for him, now that they had fallen out with the English Parliament which was not as exclusively Presbyterian as they would like, as they had been ready to fight against him four years ago. In no time at all, I had King Charles on his throne again, and England at peace. At peace. What would it be like, England at peace? I had never known it since I was old enough to notice, but it would be wondrously pleasant, with wrestling and bowling and games on the Sandhill on Sundays again. I could just remember how gay Sundays used to be. Maybe there would be players allowed into the town again. And maybe my mother would not marry Thomas Trumbell after all. And I would rebuild the fortunes of the Coles again, and maybe . . .

Suddenly I noticed tiny lights everywhere in the darkness beyond the walls, and a light rattling noise coming up out of the darkness. I scarcely had time to recognize it as the charges on musketeers' bandoleers rattling in the wind, before the alarm was given on several parts of the wall at once and the Castle's four pieces of ordnance opened up and fired the first shots in the famous storming of Tynemouth Castle.

Oh, yes, I can see you sitting up now. The old man's story has been a mite dull till now, has it? But this bit should be more lively. Well, maybe it should. The last battle of Tynemouth: and I was in it. And what can I remember of it all? A great silence. Some sounds: a little rattling noise; then the trumpets for a general alarm almost at the same moment as the trumpets for the charge from outside the walls; then a short space of noise so hideous that I can never forget it, and wish I could, of steel on steel, and steel on bone, and human voices at their ugliest and most terrible, yelling at the giving of pain, screaming at the taking of pain. And all the while a sound which I did not at first realize came from my own throat, as I struggled for my life in the dark. Some sights: first the glow-worms of the lighted matches of the musketeers springing up beyond the walls; then, the flashes of the Roundheads' muskets which suddenly seemed to appear below us from nowhere; the flashes of our own muskets as men came to the walls from all over the Castle, so few compared with the flashes from below. A few pictures were engraved on my mind forever that night: the scaling ladders brought up by the enemy; our cheers because they were too short; a short lull, and then a few flashes later the ladders miraculously grown; the gunners on the wall thrusting down with their ladles the men who came up the ladders, and who kept on coming; a flash from the cannon and two men struggling, scythe handle locked against musket butt.

In a short while there was grey light enough to see by, and suddenly there were beside me two men—I knew them both— staring motionless at each other, so alike in face that they might have been one standing in front of a looking-glass, save that only one was bald. For a second, in the flash of a musket, I saw on Harbottle Grimston's face a look of mingled love and hate impossible to describe. He muttered a few words. I did not catch their meaning but even among all the terrible sounds around there was no mistaking their note of agony. Then he was wrestling silently with the big man—it surely *was* his brother—who was slowly strangling him with his great hands, all the while chanting the field word for the night, 'For God and the King', as if it were a prayer; then a groan and a sigh as they both fell. And I thought that Harbottle Grimston's eyes showed recognition as well as pain for a moment as he stared at me across his brother's shoulder the second before they slumped down in their cruel embrace.

Then, quickly, came a fear that there could be only one end to this—a certainty that we had no chance at all. What use was my old buff coat against a sword or a musket ball, and of what avail my poor, silly scythe, which I could not even swing properly in such a close-packed mêlée, or my fists against the back and breast and gorgets of Hazelrigg's Lobsters? They were well named, and we, the wretched rabble that had rushed to Tynemouth Castle such a short time before, were as helpless as shrimps before them.

Yet I have since heard even old soldiers, who should know better, wonder how it was that Tynemouth fell so quickly—in less than an hour it was all over—and how it was that all the losses were among the defenders, contrary to the usual way in a storming. But in spite of the odds against us, I did not believe it afterwards when I heard that the enemy foot lost only one slain and one wounded, and the dragoons only two wounded— and I do not believe it yet: Hazelrigg's report to Parliament, which is all anyone knows about the storm, was a lie, to hearten Roundheads and discourage Royalists. I can still remember the hideous heaps of dead that the streaks of summer dawn began to reveal, and they were not all Royalists. Then a shout of

'Shift for yourselves' went up. I knew what that meant. Sheer panic gave me the strength to claw my way along the wall: sheer chance took me towards the Whitley Tower instead of back towards the barbican, and only the instinct for self-preservation gave me the courage and inspiration to hoist myself on to a battlement. As I turned myself round in readiness to lower myself over the wall, I saw for the last time the Great Court, and I heard the mad shouts, and I saw in the grey dawn the hideous shambles down there; and then, the second before I let go and dropped, the most hideous sight of all—the matted hair, the staring eyes, the bloody neck, as they hoisted into the air, on a pike, the head of Lieutenant-Colonel Henry Lilburne, lately Governor of Tynemouth Castle, traitor . . . or martyr.

Chapter 6

You know Tynemouth Castle, or, rather, what is left of it. You have seen the walls on the north side: you have seen how immediately below the walls steep cliffs drop down to the sea. Then perhaps *you* can hazard a guess, for I cannot, how it was that I survived my drop from the battlements, and not only survived it but received nothing worse than a few cuts and bruises. My hands were the worst; the fingers were badly scraped and tingled and burned. My last thought as I let go had been that someone might have been watching me and might be just ready to hack at my fingers with a sword: it had given me courage to let go. My first thought as I came to myself again on a little ledge fragrant with the smell of bruised tansy, was of the pain in my fingers, and for a moment I wondered if they had been injured by a sword. With that fear came another, that I had been seen going over the wall and was even now being searched for. This helped me to gather my scattered wits and forget my aching head and throbbing fingers long enough to raise myself and look around.

The whole scene was unbelievably quiet and peaceful and utterly remote from the horror of the night. I was lying on the edge of the world, between blue sky and green-blue sea, at my back a clump of tansy, yellow against golden-brown cliffs. The sun was hot and high in the heavens and I knew that I must have been lying there some hours. That was all to the good: it almost certainly meant that I had not been seen going over the wall and that I was safe here for a while, since the search for fugitives which would undoubtedly be going on at this very minute was unlikely to bring anyone to this improbable spot. Half-dazed as I still was, that was as far as I could think for the moment. I eased myself into a half-sitting, half-lying position and noticed with listless satisfaction that I could move all my limbs. I felt without alarm the dried blood on my cheek and the gash from which it had come, and drifted back into an uneasy sleep.

A cool breeze in my face and a chill striking into my bones from the rock I lay on brought me back to consciousness again.

Though I felt very stiff and cramped, I knew I was much better: my fingers still throbbed but most of my headache was gone. Moreover, I was aware of being hungry and thirsty. With clumsy fingers I fumbled in my pocket. Praise be, I still had Alyse's bread and neat's tongue, as well as some of Lilburne's bread and cheese, but nothing to drink. Now, above all, I wanted something to drink—already my tongue felt unbearably dry and large. I should have to move from the ledge to find water. In any case I could not stay here much longer. I must move before nightfall and the sun was a long way down the sky. In fact, I must begin my climb down the cliff as soon as possible, because soon shadows on the rocks would make them even more dangerous.

Before beginning the climb I forced my aching brain to think what I must do. My first idea was to get back home and hide until I could smuggle myself on board a ship, perhaps my uncle's: it was due to sail for Antwerp this week. But would not all ships leaving the Tyne be searched even more strictly than usual? And the search had been strict enough since the beginning of July, for many a gentleman of Northumberland who had been with Sir Richard Tempest had been in hiding since, waiting to find a ship to take him across to France, or the Low Countries, or anywhere out of this unhappy country.

And how could I get back home? Even supposing I could reach the city without being picked up by one of the patrols from the Castle searching for straggling fugitives, how could I get through the city gates? The pass that had taken me out of the city yesterday had my name on it—and my name was also on the muster roll in the Castle. Once that roll was examined it would not be long before the house in the Close was searched. I might face it out, of course, and swear that the Ralph Cole on the roll and the Ralph Cole of the Close were different people. I durst not risk this. Harbottle Grimston, I was convinced, had recognized me. I thought he was dead but could I be sure? And anyway, Thomas Trumbell had seen me go. So, with a sinking heart, I had to dismiss the idea of trying to get back to Newcastle.

There were still bands of Royalists in Northumberland, and Berwick was still held for the King. Should I try to reach Berwick and perhaps hope to fall in with some Cavaliers on the way? But one of the most recent rumours had been that the

Royalist Governor of Berwick had refused to admit a single soul more because he had scarcely enough food for the people already in the city. In any case, before I reached Berwick, Oliver Cromwell, who had been on his way north for so long, might finally have come to Northumberland and might be besieging Berwick itself.

Not a trace of my tiredness remained; my brain was active enough now, pouring all kinds of objections and fears into my timid heart. The sun was still farther down the sky. I must move at once and hope that when I reached—if I reached— the bottom of the cliff some plan might come to me.

The climb was easier than I expected. I had fallen down the steepest and most difficult rocks, those immediately below the walls, and to my vast relief the lower half was not much worse than some of the climbs I had undertaken with school-friends, or for the admiration of Emmet, who sometimes envied her brother's freedom. Even so, my fingers were bleeding again, my skin was clammy and my heart was pumping fast, when I slithered the last few feet and landed in a little pool with a splash and a rattle of loose stones that seemed to drown the sound of the waves themselves. I remained motionless, one part of me noticing that the water was still warm from the sun, a bigger part of me waiting for the rattle of stones to stop and for the shout from the Castle that would show I had been seen. At last there was only the wet slap of the incoming waves in the little gullies among the rocks and the dry scraping noise of the spent waves retreating.

I could pause here, but only for a moment. These rocks, I knew, were covered at high tide. During my short wakeful period in the afternoon, I had not thought to notice where the tide was and so I had no way of knowing immediately whether it was coming in or going out. It was probably coming in, I thought: the rocks just under the cliff seemed dry. But it did not really matter as there was no question of spending the night here. I must get away from the neighbourhood of the Castle and I must find some water to drink. My throat and tongue were so parched and swollen that I was almost tempted to kneel and lap the salt-water in the rock pool.

Suddenly, as I stared at the red anemones and green weed in the pool, a plan sprang, ready-made, into my head. It was by no means perfect, but it seemed the most hopeful so far. True, it involved working my way round the Castle and over a mile or more of country where there were sure to be patrols, but almost any plan would do that, because the only other way to go would take me where I did not want to go—northwards, away from the Tyne. Berwick I had already decided against. Morpeth? It was in the hands of the Roundheads. Alnwick? Heaven only knew who held Alnwick. What else was there? Nothing but a few villages where a new-comer would be suspected at once. No, my only hope, I decided rapidly, lay in getting over the dangerous mile or so in the immediate neighbourhood of the Castle, and making for the Cole salt-pans. Once there, I would throw myself on the mercy—and the cupidity—of Will Reaveley and the others. Fortunately for me, the number of workers at the pans had dwindled steadily of recent years and months. Those still employed would be old servants of the Coles. I hoped to persuade them to let me stay among them and work like one of them until the hue and cry died down. It would be fairly simple for a message to be taken to my mother and she might, before the end of the sailing season, be able to get me on to a collier or a merchant ship going to Europe.

My spirits began to rise now that I knew what I was going to do. I decided that although the distance to the salt-pans would be shorter if I went south across the rocks, around the point and into Prior's Haven, this route would be too dangerous, since the Haven might very well have Parliament ships at anchor there. I must therefore work my way northwards, into the little sandy bay known to the fisherfolk as the Short Sands. I should have to keep as close as possible to the bottom of the cliffs because the bay could be seen from the Castle, from the Whitley Tower and the north wall that I had escaped by, and also from the fishermen's cottages whose red roofs flowered above the grassy slopes which took the place of cliffs in the middle of the bay.

I set off as quickly as my stiff limbs would allow, sometimes slithering through the mud washed down to the cliff base by that wet summer, sometimes grazing and bumping myself on the great boulders that were never wet except in winter storms. Once I had to wade through the noisome debris of an outlet from a Castle *garde-robe*.

They say that there is a special providence that watches over drunkards and fools: most assuredly I was a very big fool for only a special providence had taken me over the wall without breaking my neck. Now I had another amazing piece of good fortune. Just as I was rounding the rocks and coming into the bay, I noticed drifting over the water the first wisps of that sea-fret which so often spoils the end of a warm summer day on that coast. I halted for a moment to breathe a formless prayer that the fret would develop and roll inland.

It did. By the time I had reached the bottom of the steep grassy slopes, my hair and eyelashes were sticky with salty mist, and I could hardly see an arm's length in front of me. If the fret lasted, I had a fair chance of getting safely past the Castle.

First I had to find a way up the grass cliff. There must be a path of some sort. The fishermen might use Prior's Haven for their cobles, but their children played on these sands and I had in times past seen their women shrimping on the rocks. I went down on my knees and crawled along, straining to peer through the mist, and groping with my hands for a break in the grass that might be a track. At last I felt, and saw, a bare rock which had been roughly hewn into a step, and I heard myself grunt with triumph. Very carefully I felt my way: even with the aid of the primitive path it was not easy to climb in the mist. In places the steps were treacherous with mud and once they petered out altogether, and for a panic-stricken moment I thought I should have to climb the rest of the way—and in the mist I had lost all sense of how much farther that would be— as best I could over slippery grass. Then, groping desperately around, I found that the steps had not ceased, they had just taken a sharp turn to the left.

I was sobbing for breath when at last I stumbled on to the level grass at the top of the cliff and my thirst had been so increased by my exertions that I actually thought of going to ask for a drink at one of the cottages. I did not entertain the idea for long. The fewer folk who had seen a strange boy near the Castle the better. I must endure my thirst a while longer. Food I had but I knew it would stick in my throat, so I rested only long enough for my labouring breath to become calm again before picking up my weary self once more.

On the cliff top the sea-fret was not as thick as lower down and at water level. It was still creeping in, but unevenly. There were patches through which it was easily possible to see and be seen. It was not so thick that I should lose my way (after all I knew the district well enough) but it did hide me from the view of all except any search-parties I might meet at close quarters. There was a real risk that I might do this. Hazelrigg would not be satisfied simply with taking the Castle: he would spare no effort to round up all its Royalist garrison. Parliament was determined to root out all its opponents in this new war. It had been merciful to its defeated enemies, before; this time they were not going to be allowed to escape to make still further trouble. Anyone who took up arms for the King in 1648 knew what to expect. If he were an old Parliament man who had changed his side, he could expect no mercy—death awaited him. If he were an old Royalist, or if he had not fought at all before, Parliament would be more merciful: he would be sold—yes, sold—to a merchant, marched to a port and thence shipped within fourteen days either to the plantations in Barbados, or to Venice to spend the rest of his days at the Venetian galleys. In either case his days would not be very numerous. Enterprising merchants who bought military prisoners from Parliament and made a good profit out of disposing of them were rumoured to give a small proportion of their gains to individual zealous Roundhead officers who had a good score of captured Royalists. What Parliament man could be blamed for earning a little useful extra money when his pay was always in arrears—especially if he was serving God at the same time? I shivered, and wondered how I and so many men could have been mad enough to forget all these things.

I had stood there in indecision too long. I must not be taken prisoner, that was all. And from now on I would act no more on impulse. I started to walk forward. As I have already said, the mist was patchy now. Ahead of me, on my left, I could just make out the Castle, strangely remote in its veils of mist; on the right was the straggling street of cottages that made up the main part of Tynemouth village. The shortest way to the salt-pans was immediately past the front of the Castle, but now that I could see its threatening walls again, I knew that this was a way I could not take. The sun was setting now: the villagers would certainly be, if not in bed, at least wisely indoors. It would be safer to go away from the Castle, past the village. It was no good hanging about in this uncertain fashion: that was the surest way to arouse suspicion in anyone who did chance to see me. I must appear as if I had every right to be in Tyne-mouth village. What I should do if anyone challenged me I had not the slightest idea: cudgel my brains as I might, I could not think of any reason I could give for my presence there.

So it was with a thumping heart that I walked, trying not to move too cautiously, nor too quickly, nor yet too noisily, to-wards the cottages on my right, turning my back on the Castle.

There was no sign of life beyond the faint glimmer of a rushlight in one or two of the cottages. I went the whole length of the street, then was past the village, and my breath was coming more easily. I was wondering if I could now safely turn south towards the river when suddenly my feet shot from under me and I was sprawling among a spitting, scratching cluster of fiends from hell itself, that set up a chorus of angry howls and fled, screeching, in all directions. In a second the sickening smell and the slithering slime beneath my fingers told me where I was: I had stumbled into the village midden which—to judge by its appalling stench—contained the rotting guts of all the fish that had ever been taken out of the sea.

I stumbled my way out. The noise made by those foraging cats was loud enough not only to awaken the whole village but to rouse the Castle guards as well. All thoughts of caution gone, I took to my heels and ran till my bursting lungs forced me to stop and I flung myself down in a little hollow, gulping at the raw air as if I could never have enough.

At last breathing ceased to be painful. I listened. Not a sound came through the mist, only the beating of my own blood in my ears. My panic began to seem foolish: the sound of cats fighting over offal was commonplace anywhere. I felt a trifle ashamed of my terror—no more acting on impulse I had decided, remember—as my pulses quietened and the stillness soaked into me. I even began to notice the nauseating smell of my hands and clothes.

There was not much light left in the sky now, but enough for me to catch a glimmer at the bottom of the hollow. It was a little marshy pool, scarcely bigger than a plate, but enough to soothe my swollen tongue. I lay on my stomach and drank.

The water put new heart into me, and when I could drink no more, I wiped my hands as clean as might be, and pulled a fistful of moist grass and scrubbed the worst of the stinking offal from my clothes.

I was pleased to find that the food in my pocket had escaped contamination and dry though they were, the scraps of bread and tongue and the morsel of cheese which I allowed myself before getting on to my feet again were fine fare to me.

The sky had more light on my right than on my left, so I judged that, even in my panic, I had run in the direction of the river mouth. I listened intently. All was quiet. But it was very difficult to see now: there was still mist about, and the after-light of the sun's setting was no longer rosy, but very grey. It must have been much later than I had realized when I climbed down from the ledge below the Castle walls. Ought I to try to find my way to the salt-pans tonight, or would it be wiser to find a hiding-place somewhere near by? That should not be difficult: there must be plenty of derelict mine-shafts in the neighbourhood. It would be no harder to climb down one than down the cliff face, and if I were lucky enough to come across a really old working, not as far to the bottom. A second's thought, however, was enough to show that to attempt to climb down an unknown sinking, in the dark, was a crazy scheme: and, anyway, I was not desperate enough—yet—to spend a night down in the earth, alone with Heaven knew what strange devils.

So I scrambled rather stiffly out of the little hollow. I felt better now that my thirst had been slaked, though the lesser pains in fingers, elbows, and knees could now claim my attention, and withal fairly cheerful.

I could walk at only a moderate pace for I was afraid, in the dark and mist, of falling into an open mine-shaft. Most coal-owners saw no reason, when workings were abandoned, to throw good money after bad by sealing them off.

How far I had gone I could not tell for I had lost all count of time and distance, but my hopes were rising with every step that took me away from the Castle when suddenly a sound made my heart miss a beat and then race twice as hard. It was only the sound of voices, men's voices, but it froze me where I stood. I could not make out what they were saying, but surely they were coming nearer. And they carried torches. In a moment I should be able to see them—and they me. They were only a few steps behind me. My limbs were unlocked: I started to run. The mist shifted.

'There's another of them,' a voice shouted.

'Stop in the name of Parliament,' cried another.

The ground was sloping rapidly downwards: I slithered and ran. And kept on running. The shouts grew more distant: I was shaking off my pursuers. I might be safe yet. The thought had hardly formed, when I ran straight into the arms of a soldier who had been quietly waiting at the bottom of the slope.

'Got him!' he shouted. 'I'll fetch him up, sergeant,' and, holding my arm in a vicious grip, he started to force me back up the hill to where the others were waiting. By the light of the torches I could see they were most of them troopers, but in their midst two sorry-looking wretches were roped together. I could not bear to look at them.

I was near tears, from the cruel disappointment of being taken, but I tried to put a bold face on things.

'Let go of me: you're hurting my arm,' I said.

'You'll smart a bit more afore you're done,' he answered. 'Son of the bottomless pit! Rebel! Traitor!'

Rebel, traitor ... the hypocrite. He was the traitor—traitor to the anointed King. How could anyone be a traitor to Parliament, men elected by men, not chosen by God?

'Traitor! I'm no traitor!' I shouted. My anger was so real that the trooper, for a second, just a second, wondered if he could have made a mistake. I could feel his doubt, the momentary slackening of his grip. That gave me my chance. I wrenched myself free and turned and once more raced down the slope with no other thought in my head than to run faster than the men behind me.

Now I had reached the bottom of the hill and was splashing through a tiny burn. My speed was slackening: the ground was rising and the slope dragged at my footsteps. The shouts grew nearer again. My breath was almost gone; my legs strangely weak. It was no use: I must give up. I fell, sobbing, to my knees. Then, my hands, clutching at grass and gorse, closed miraculously on a stone, a wet, smooth, regular stone, slimy with the ooze of years. My fingers did my thinking for me: of their own accord they felt along the stone. My fingers were right. I hauled myself past the gorse that screened it, over the cold wet pebbles, through the narrow opening; and lay still, trying to hush my labouring breath. I was safe.

Chapter 7

I dragged myself far enough into the adit to be out of sight and lay there, my lungs shuddering, my heart beating as if it would burst. The gorse bushes could not have stopped moving after I had pushed through them, when I heard the sound of feet and then of voices which stopped just outside. I tried to quieten my labouring breath, which, in that narrow space, seemed loud enough to betray me. I listened, taut with fear.

'Nay, he can't be far. Confound this mist. Stop and listen a minute.'

There was only the rustle of the stiff bushes: the men must be at the very entrance of the adit, only inches away.

A silence followed.

'He must be hereabouts. There's not a sound. Must be hiding. He cannot have got away from us: he had only a few yards start. Let's search around. We'll take these bushes: you take those.'

'Don't be daft, man. How could he hide in those stunted things? They're half starved like the rest of us. This fret's better cover than them tonight. Come on, man, he'll be in Shields before you've stopped gabbin'.'

Another voice joined in now; I could not catch what it said, but the first man must have been persuaded, because the troopers seemed to be moving away. I listened anxiously. The voices and movements became fainter and in a very short time I could hear nothing. I durst not make a move yet: they could still be quite near and I not hear them. I must wait until I could be sure they were not searching for me in the neighbourhood of the adit before I crawled out again into the cool night air. I was already beginning to feel suffocated in that narrow tunnel. Yet when would it be safe to leave it? The Roundheads would realize before long that they had lost me and might retrace their steps and search the bushes after all. Moreover, there might be other parties of searchers between me and the comparative safety of the salt-pans. I was beginning to think that the idea which I had dismissed earlier, of hiding in old mine workings, might be a solution after all. I had some food with me and there was a trickle of water in the adit; if I crawled forward through the opening into the mine itself, I could stay there for two or three days, and by then, surely, the search for Royalists would be less intensive. Objections to this plan crowded into my brain, but I refused to listen to them: I could find no better plan—that was the deciding factor.

Yet it was a long while before I forced myself to begin to crawl farther into the adit. It may seem to you a less dangerous thing to do than to drop over the Castle walls on to a steep cliff, but that I had done in the heat and terror of battle, after seeing bloody scenes which showed me all too clearly what my own fate could be. Now I was alone, and cold, bitterly cold, and utterly weary; but at last I drove myself to begin to crawl along farther into the hill-side, farther into a darkness so solid that it seemed to weigh on my eyes.

I say that I began to crawl along the adit, but crawl is not really the right word. Rather, I pressed myself along: there was not space enough to crawl. By an agonizing straining of every muscle in my body, which somehow concentrated power in fingers, shoulders, knees, and toes, I dragged myself along, inch by painful inch. Not only was I hindered by the narrowness of the tunnel, but the stones were slimy and there was a slow trickle of water all the time. The fears I had rejected before clamoured to be heard now. The adit might grow narrower; or, long disused, it might be blocked by a fall of stone from its roof: it would be even harder to go back than to go forward. Then came the terrible fear that by now the sea-fret might have turned into rain, as it sometimes did, and the rain, even at that very moment, might be steadily seeping into the ground and gathering into the mine from all sides, at any minute turning the gentle trickle of water into a flood which would rise and drown me. All the hazards of coal-mining which hitherto had been items to put on the loss side of the family ledgers suddenly became terrifyingly personal.

I was growing hot from my exertions and my body felt as if it were growing larger. The worst fear of all fell on me now, the fear of being wedged in that tunnel, unable either to go on or to go back, forced to stay there to die slowly, alone in the dark where no one would ever find me. The grip in which I had held my fears slackened: I screamed in pure terror, and I heard myself babbling prayers with no more words than, 'Please God, please God,' and, over and over again, 'Mother, Mother.'

At last, terror brought its own cure, exhaustion. How long I lay there, immobilized by fear, I do not know. It may have been hours, it may have been only moments; they were, I believe, the worst moments of my life, but like all other moments they passed; a kind of strained calm followed, and I was able to go on.

I pulled myself on and on, interminably; I was prepared now to go on for ever. Then, the air was warmer. My fingers still clutched stone, but the pressure had gone from my shoulders: I clawed my way forward with a sudden access of strength. At the same moment as I knew that I had reached the end of the adit, I saw will-o'-the-wisp glimmers of light, heard an eerie screech. I ought to have been afraid for it seemed to me that I had stumbled on one of those nests of fiends that are hidden in the coal-pits. But I was too exhausted for fear: I lay where I was, half clear of the adit and—I swear it—fell asleep.

Chapter 8

It was the sound of voices—human voices—that woke me. I could not think where I was, my body lying on rough, cold ground, my head on rough, warm cloth, and tepid water trickling down my chin, so that for a second I thought I was back in the adit again.

'Hold on, hold on, man. Divn't choke the lad,' a voice was saying. 'He's coming to, anyway.'

I struggled to sit up. I seemed to be in a circle of lights that did not stay still but bobbed up and down and from side to side all the time. I saw that they were candles, sputtering, tallow candles whose pungent reek caught at my throat. At first I looked at the candles and could see only their light, then I looked past them and as my eyes adjusted themselves I saw that each candle was stuck in a blob of damp clay, which, in its turn, was stuck on to a shiny leather cap. Below each cap I could just make out a grimy face, with flashes of white eyeballs, or white teeth.

Of course ... they were pitmen. Why had I been so sure that my adit would lead to an abandoned pit? If I had been capable of thinking I should have realized that it was in too good a condition to lead to a disused working. The men stared at me and I stared at them; and the pillars of coal behind them glittered in the candlelight.

Now another voice was speaking, a voice harder than the first one, and with a note of authority in it.

'Well, come on, hurry up. What's all this? Let's be having an account of you. What fetched you here like that, scaring the wits out of the lot of them?' There was a trace of scorn in his voice as well as impatience. I learnt later that when I had suddenly appeared at the mouth of the adit, the man working nearest to it (how had I not heard the sound of picks as I had come towards them?) had dropped his pick and made for the eye, yelling to the others that the Devil was among them. For some seconds there had been a wild scramble to the eye, but Kit Sanderson—he it was who had just spoken to me—who was afraid of neither man nor devil, had gone to investigate the apparition and had rated the rest in no uncertain terms for being cowards as well as fools.

'Well, come on.' He shook me: he was growing impatient. Still I hesitated. He must have guessed what was in my mind for he went on, 'It'd just as well be the truth, lad. I suppose you're one of the fools they're out hunting for right now?'

I nodded. Then I grabbed his arm and was going to beg him not to give me away. He removed my hand from his arm.

'Nay, I'll not hand you over. What's Parliament ever done for the likes of me?' He paused, then spat. 'Or the King either. So I'll not be helping you, neither. You'd best be on your way. Archie here'll send you up to day with the next lot of corves.'

The others seemed to agree with him. Even if they had not, I doubt whether they would have argued with him.

'At least let me stay here today.' I was ashamed of the quaver in my voice, but try as I might I could not keep it steady.

He did not answer. I started fumbling in my innermost pocket.

'I've got some money: I can pay you,' I said.

He gave me a look, half-scornful, half-pitying.

'Nay, lad,' he said, 'what makes you think we'd risk the plantations for owt you could pay us? Anyway,' he went on, 'what's to stop us taking your money and giving you up all the same? Now, come on, hinnie, the sooner you're out of here the better for the lot of us. There's mebbe men out searching all the pits round the Castle, working or not working. Hazelrigg's out to get every man Jack of you. If you're still here when they search *my* pit,' here a note of pride crept into his voice, 'there'll be no lies told for you. Now, come on, there's a good lad, it's no use arguing. Count yourself lucky we're letting you go so easy.' He turned away from me and took up his pick. 'Back to work, marras. There's been enough time wasted already.'

Lucky! To go up into the daylight (it must be day by now) and walk straight into the arms of another search troop! I could never hope to reach the salt-pans in broad daylight. The whole idea had been quite crazy. I ought to have gone north as fast as I could.

Yet the beginnings of an idea were forming in my mind, an idea which had begun to stir when I had noticed the change in his voice when he said 'my pit'.

'No, wait a minute. Listen. I could be useful to you,' I said, desperately grabbing his arm again. I saw his look of impatience. 'No, I don't mean what you're thinking. Does the name Cole mean anything to you? Yes, it must, if you're a coal-owner.' I used the words 'coal-owner' to flatter him: a man who worked in his own pit scarcely deserved the title. But if he was not in coal in a small way, my offer was not going to tempt him. The words started to pour out now, as if this were an old, old scheme, not one which was taking shape at the same moment as the words that expressed it. 'Look, my name is Cole, Ralph Cole, Ralph Cole of the Close.' I saw that he was interested, but not really believing. 'Yes, it is. Look I'll prove it to you.' I found and thrust into his hand the pass for leaving and re-entering Newcastle which was still, miraculously, in my pocket.

He took it and peered at it in the flickering light of the candles. A doubt whether he could read crossed my mind, but he said, 'All right, so you're Ralph Cole. Of the Close. But we're only giving you a minute, Ralph Cole.' There was a trace of a sneer in his voice as he repeated my name.

'You called this *your* pit, just now. *Is* it yours?' I asked. He nodded, and so did the other pitmen, who seemed content to leave the talking to him. 'Now my guess is that you got hold of this pit, somehow, after 1644. Right? Now I don't know how you've kept it going so long: most of the men who got these little pits then have found they couldn't make a go of them. I'll lay any money it's not been easy.'

They were all listening intently now.

'How've you been getting rid of your coal? To the salt-pans? By land sale, hereabouts?' I went on.

'Nay, if you're one of them hostmen lot, you know fine well that's all we're let do.' There was hostility in the man's voice now.

'I *thought* so. There's nowt to be made out of that, now is there?' I paused.

'There's a bare living,' he said, 'but that'll be nowt to a hostman's son, I'll wand.'

He had led us to the point where I wanted to be.

'All right, then. How'd you like to sell your coal through a hostman and join the sea-sale of coal?'

I thought this would be a winning stroke but to my surprise

their tense faces relaxed and plain incredulity mixed with rueful amusement took over.

'I'd like it fine,' said one, 'and I'd like fine to fly.' He turned to his friends. 'Come on, marras, we'll get shot of him and get started work again.'

They were even prepared to be hostile now, but their leader, Kit Sanderson, was looking thoughtful.

'Hold on,' he said. 'We'll hear what the lad's got to say.'

He had given me my chance: it was for me now to persuade him. I told them that I was the son of the hostman Nicholas Cole, who was killed at the siege of Newcastle; that my mother had been allowed by both the Committee of Parliament in Newcastle and the Hostmen's Guild to carry on his trade as coal-owner and coal-fitter. I was her only son and although she must be very angry with me, I knew, *I knew* that she would be ready to help me by striking some kind of bargain with them. If they would agree to keep me hidden until the hunt for fugitives was called off, she would agree to find some way of selling their coal for them far more profitably than they could themselves.

'How?' said one of them bluntly.

'Oh, never mind how,' I answered impatiently: it seemed easy enough to me, coming of a hostman's family, but they had never been in that privileged position. 'There are always ways and means of colouring coal.'

'That I'll believe,' said Kit, 'but what I want to know is how can we be sure that she'll make a bargain to colour ours, and, more important, stick to it?'

'You can't. You'll just have to gamble on it,' I was forced to admit, and I see-sawed down into hopelessness again. Yet, if I had been an old hand at bargaining, I could not have given a better answer, for, though I did not know it then, every miner is a natural-born gambler. Moreover, Kit would not have asked the question if he had not been already three parts won over. Long afterwards he told me that he had never really hesitated, because, for the second time in his life, he felt he was being given a chance to force his way into the ranks of the privileged. The first chance he had seized when he had bullied and cajoled his friends into sinking their tiny savings in this venture when, in 1644, there were, for the first time in his life, pits to be had by men like him. The gradual discovery that the coal trade was, in spite of Parliament's victory, still in the grip of the hostmen—'same Guild, just a few new faces'—and that they would never be allowed a part in the profitable side of coal, the coastwise trade with London and the Continent, would have broken up the little group of venturers had a man of less fanatical determination to succeed been their leader. Kit had kept them together, working as hard as any two of them, inspiring them with some of his certainty that these were times when some of the old men must go down and new men come up, and waiting for his chance, for the opening, the crack in the wall of privilege, which would let him through. 'And you, Ralph, were my chance, though such a queer-looking chance, when you tumbled through that adit, that I didn't recognize you at first.'

The others never would have recognized their chance: there was grumbling before he talked them into accepting me as one of them, at least until he had been to Newcastle and seen my mother. It was finally agreed that I should stay there and work with them until their stint for the day was done. If we were questioned either in the pit or up on top, I was Kit's young brother, not over-bright in the head.

I was all for Kit's going immediately to Newcastle and seeing my mother that day, but he would have none of it. They would do as few things out of the ordinary as possible that day, so we should leave the pit together at the usual time. Kit did risk going to the top of the shaft to explain what was happening to the two remaining members of the venture, the surface-workers, the winder and the riddler. They had to be told because they would be the first to be questioned if searchers did come to our pit, and they must give the right number if they were asked how many men were working underground. I was told the men's names before we started to work but the only ones I can remember now are Kit Sanderson and Archie Reede.

I spent the rest of the day working as a hurrier. I was given this job because it was the least skilled and because an extra hurrier would be useful. They were short-handed even for such a little pit. Underground there were only four hewers and one hurrier (in some pits the hurrier is called a putter). Because the four hewers cut more coal than one hurrier could deal with, they used to stop hewing from time to time when the coal was piling up and help the hurrier to load his corves and drag them to the eye. When the winder could not get the corves to the surface fast enough, one of the hewers would go up to day and help there. It was, as I said, a very small venture, and I soon discovered that all the men would give a hand wherever it was needed.

That day I had my first experience of hard manual work and I have never forgotten it. It was stifling hot in the pit—I should have thought that the farther away from the sun the colder it would be—and even before starting work I was glad to strip off my doublet and shirt. My white skin was startlingly different from the others' black bodies. Any Parliament man descending the shaft would have picked me out at once. It was not long, however, before I was as grimy as the rest. Piling the coals on to a corf and dragging the corf to the shaft was heavier work than I had ever done in my life before: in a few minutes I was steaming with sweat and black with coal-dust which settled in my hair, clung to my skin, and made my eyes smart long before the day was over. My arms ached, my back was sore, and I was gasping like a broken-winded horse.

'Nay, lad, there's no need to go at it like a bull at a gate,' said Archie Reede, my fellow putter, before long. 'You'll not can last the day out that road. Take it slow and steady like me.'

I felt a little sheepish: I had been deliberately trying to get more corves to the eye than he, just to show what I could do. During the discussion whether to let me stay or not doubts had been cast on my usefulness. 'More bother than he'll be worth,' and 'He'll just get in the road,' were two opinions that were rankling.

We were loading coal from Kit Sanderson's board when Archie said this.

'Time to knock off for a bit, anyway,' said Kit. 'Time for bait,' he called to the others.

The men all left their work and went and sat at the eye. During the time I worked in the pit I noticed that the farther away they were from the eye the more uneasy the men were. It was safest at the eye and the air most wholesome. When I came to know all the hazards of their life, I learnt to admire pitmen. Even a soldier does not risk his life every day: a miner does. I know they are always being blamed for being gamblers and spendthrifts. How could they not be gamblers with money when they gamble their lives in the ordinary business of earning their bread? As for their being spendthrift, the charge is most commonly made by men who spend as much on their wine and tobacco as the miner earns for the whole living of himself and his wife and bairns. So you can see it was a good thing for me that I never did take over the Cole estate. Had I never been more than that one day in a pit, I still could not afterwards have made a successful coal-owner—I knew what it was like to be a coal worker.

The men had collected their leather water-bottles and their bundles of food from the worked-out board nearest the eye. At first they were shy about offering me a drink and a 'bite' of their food, it 'not being what you're used to', but when they saw the sorry state of my tired packet of food, they lost some of their diffidence. They were rough but kind, and having once agreed to accept me, did their best for me. But, in spite of their kindness, we had not a lot to say to each other: their natural good manners prevented them from asking me questions about myself, I was too shy to volunteer information, and we had no shared experience to talk about. I sat and tried to keep out thoughts of home by listening to their conversation. They did give me some news about the war, but mostly what I knew or had guessed already. The Royalist garrison at Tynemouth had been almost completely routed; Lilburne was dead; Newcastle was still in the hands of Parliament; the Scots had not yet come to the aid of Royalists in Northumberland—they were believed to be still in Cumberland—though the most recent rumour was that they had joined Sir Marmaduke Langdale's forces and might be in Lancashire. Lieutenant-General Cromwell was on his way out of Wales and would presently join the Major-General Lambert to attack the Scots and the English Royalists in the North so that they could march to Newcastle. One item was news to me—that Scarborough Castle also had revolted against Parliament and, unlike Tynemouth, was still being held for the King. But they really had very little to say about the war, perhaps because they were not very interested in it, or perhaps out of consideration for my feelings, because clearly the King's cause was going very badly. They seemed to be mainly interested in pigeons and dogs, whose finer points they were prepared to discuss interminably.

Kit Sanderson brought the break to an end. When he

started to get up, the rest followed suit without interrupting their conversation and, apparently, without even having noticed his move. Back to work we went: each hewer to his own board and Archie Reede and I to our muscle-straining job of loading and dragging the corves. It was so utterly different from anything I had ever known before that I felt it was not I but a stranger who knelt and heaved big lumps of coal into the corves or scooped up the smaller stuff with hands bruised and grazed, and whose limbs had developed an obstinate will of their own which kept their aching owner moving when he could have cried from tiredness. I was too tired even to want to stop when the next break came in case I should not be able to start again.

I was too exhausted to feel nervous when the moment came, at last, to leave the pit, and Archie who had taken me under his kindly wing, showed me how to put my leg and knee in the noose at the end of the rope hanging down the shaft, and the kind of grip to use to hold the rope with my right arm. 'Be sure to keep your left arm free to give yourself a push if you start scraping the wall too much,' he said. It was Archie who gave the signal on the rope to the winder to start the old donkey going to draw up the rope. 'And mind you keep him slow and steady for the lad,' he bellowed up the shaft, though whether the winder could hear him seemed doubtful. But I woke up quickly enough when the rope sagged suddenly and terrifyingly as it took my weight, and the noose tightened on my leg, and I started to revolve and bump against the rough side of the shaft, which was only about four feet wide. The nightmare was not long, however, and I emerged into day at last.

It had been decided some time during the working hours to drop the idea of passing me off as Kit Sanderson's brother. As the leader of the venture he was fairly well known in those parts and he was the man most likely to be questioned. Archie Reede was a younger man and a bachelor with least to lose if he were found harbouring a fugitive Royalist; also, as one of the others said, he was handy with his fists and a good runner into the bargain. Not that that would be much help to either him or me if we were found out: our only hope lay in not arousing any suspicions. Archie had agreed to take me with him, in the most ordinary manner possible, so that it hardly occurred to me to be grateful to him for the risk he was taking.

A grimy old jerkin had been found for me: my buff doublet might make me conspicuous among them, and it might just possibly have been noticed, dark though it had been at the time of my encounter with the search-party. So I was quite indistinguishable from the other pitmen as, drunk with fatigue, I stumbled along the muddy lane to the row of little cottages where Archie, Kit Sanderson, and two of the other men had their homes. Scarcely a conscious thought stirred in the vast need for sleep which filled me.

Archie led me round the back of the cottages, where there was a sort of communal yard with a large midden and two privies on the far side, and beyond these some patches of garden with one or two hen-crees. The yard was a morass after the wet summer we had had. A path of smooth sea-pebbles ran the length of the yard, past the backdoors of the cottages. One behind the other we crunched along it, ducking and twisting to avoid wooden tubs and buckets hanging on nails near the doors, until, having said good night to Kit and the others, Archie and I reached the last cottage of all. Its white walls were gay with the evening light and with nasturtiums growing as neatly as nasturtiums ever could over a tiny porch made, I should have guessed, from driftwood. Archie carefully cleaned his boots on the scraper outside: then he went into the porch. He took off his grimy-black leather jacket, his coal-dusty hoggers, and his leather knee-pads, and hung them on nails there, and he showed me where to hang my dusty jerkin. Then, at last, he unlatched the door and went in, calling to me to follow.

It was dark, after the pink evening outside, but as I hesitated just inside the door, suddenly shy again, I could see that it was a tiny room I found myself in, with rough whitewashed walls, and an earth floor stamped hard with sea-pebbles. Opposite the door was one narrow window, high in the wall and without glass, of course, but with a leather curtain to drop across it to keep out wind and weather. Near the door was a ladder to the sleeping loft above.

The first thing Archie did was to poke the banked up fire back into life. Then he lit a rushlight at the fire and stuck it in a holder on the shelf above the fire-place. By its smoky, malodorous light, I could see that the room contained a rough wooden table, some stools, two food bins, and a high-backed oak settle which served, no doubt, as a clothes-chest, and on occasion probably as a bed, as well as a draught-excluding fireside seat. The fire-place was the only remarkable feature of the room. It took up almost the whole of one wall and was made of rough brown stone, hewn, not many years before, from some neighbouring cliff. (It was clear that Archie was a man of parts and mighty houseproud.) The hearth was very big and in the middle of it, under the chimney opening, there was actually an iron grate—crudely made, but nevertheless an iron grate—in which a coal fire was smouldering sulphurously. There were two cauldrons, a large and a small, slung over the fire from a metal rail which ran above the fire from one inside wall of the fire-place to the other. I had never seen such a large fire-place or such a large fire in a poor man's house before, but of course Archie was a pitman and coal was the one comfort most pitmen had.

The next thing he did was to take down a pair of old bellows from a hook at the end of the fire-place and blaze up the fire.

'There, that's a bit more like,' he said, thriftily extinguishing the rushlight.

And indeed, with the comfortable blaze dancing on the hearth and throwing light almost to the far wall, the tiny room was the most cheerful and the most welcoming place I had seen since I had set off on my mad venture.

'First we'll have some of this muck off,' he went on. 'Then we'll have a bite and a sup. And by then you'll be ready for your bed, I'll awand.'

Then he disappeared through the door and returned a moment later with a big, round, wooden tub which he placed in front of the fire. I made a move to help him.

'Nay, lad, you can give us a hand later on. You just have a bit quiet sit now.'

I was too tired to insist. He disappeared again. This time he was gone longer. When he returned he was carrying two buckets of water. He emptied one into the tub; then he got a big ladle and started ladling water from the big cauldron into the tub; then he replenished the cauldron with the water from the second bucket. Then, in no time at all, with a sigh of pleasure he was in the tub. For a moment he enjoyed the comfort of the warm water, and then he was rubbing away as much as he could of the day's grime. He had no soap but just pounded away at his skin with a piece of coarse cloth. And all the time he talked, partly perhaps to put me at my ease but partly telling me things it might be useful for me to know. He told me that he came from Elsdon, the gathering place for the clans of the Middle Marches. His mother still lived there—his father had been dead these ten years—and he went to see her each winter when the coal trade was slack and men were laid off. No, he had no brothers and sisters—'except you, Ralph'. No, he didn't know Jackie Armstrong: it was a long while since Jackie had been back to Elsdon. But he knew Jackie's sister. And he told me a lot about Kit Sanderson, and a little about the other members of the venture.

When he was dressed again, this time in the simple everyday dress of a workman, I could at last get a good look at him—he had until then been only white teeth, and blue eyes and a pleasant voice. I liked what I saw. It was not a remarkable face: nondescript features; commonplace nose; inconspicuous (but not weak) chin; mouth neither very large nor very small; skin rather sallow but a faint dusting of freckles survived over his cheekbones. His eyes even looked less blue now that most of the coal grime had been removed, and his teeth less white. But it was a kind, friendly face.

'Nay, but you'll know us the next time you see us, Ralph, lad,' he said, and laughed at my little jump of embarrassment. 'Come on, your turn now. You can give us a hand with emptying this tub.'

We had almost emptied the tub and were, one at each side, gingerly tilting it over a bucket to let the last of the water run out, when a loud hammering at the door startled us, so that we almost knocked the bucket over. We stared at each other over the curve of the tub; then, as the hammering was repeated, Archie, with a grim face, motioned me towards the shadows at the farthest side of the fire-place, and picking up the bucket of dirty water was on his way to the door, when the hammering gave way to a fumbling as the latch was discovered, and the door flung open. Into the room burst a troop of soldiers, who collided with Archie; the bucket was knocked out of his hand and water was splashed over him and over the first of the invaders. There was no need for play-acting: Archie really meant the words of abuse that burst from him. But an officer was pushing his way forward from the door and a harsh voice was saying, 'Hold your peace, profane man, lest God strike you dumb.'

I had heard that voice before: and even in the half-darkness my unwilling eyes recognized that huge, menacing bulk. It could not be, but it was, Harbottle Grimston.

Chapter 9

He was paler than usual, perhaps, and the edge of a bandage showed at his throat, but he seemed as arrogant as ever. I must surely have imagined his moment of pain when he struggled with his brother.

The spilt water had made a mess of Archie's stockings and shoes, and the fluster of annoyance that he was making gave us both a moment to recover ourselves somewhat and prepare to face the questions that must follow. Archie's turn came first.

His name?

Archie Reede.

Yes, this was his home, leastways in summer; in winter,

when most of the pits were shut, he sometimes went back to Elsdon, to see his mother.

This provoked insulting remarks about mosstroopers that made Archie grit his teeth, but he kept his temper.

He had been working on the Tyne for six years now. Yes, anybody round here could bear out his story.

Where had he been on the day of August the ninth?

When was that? The day before yesterday: well, where should he have been but down the pit?

And where had he been the night of August the eighth?

In his bed where he ought to be.

Yes, he had heard guns over by the Castle.

No, he had not got up to find out what was happening; he was too fond of his neck to stick it into quarrels that had nowt in them but misery for poor folk like him.

Archie was unmoved by Harbottle Grimston's tirade on the sacred duty of every true son of Israel to smite the Hittites hip and thigh.

No, he had not seen any fugitives come this way.

Yes, he knew what the punishment was for harbouring escaped enemies of Parliament.

Who was that with him? That was his younger brother, doing his first season in the pit. Yes, go ahead, question him, though they'd not get much out of him: he was not over-bright in the head, which was why he was so old starting in the pit—his mother had kept him at home a bit longer.

Yes, search the place: there was only one room apart from the one they were in: the ladder was over there. But he hoped they'd be quick about it and give him and the lad a chance to clean up and get a bite to eat. They'd had a hard day, if nobody else had.

Archie stood up to the questioning very well: he was neither too eager to please, nor too unwilling to answer.

The spilt water; the water still heating over the fire; Archie's newly-washed skin with its permanent greyish tinge of the regular pitman; my sweaty griminess which hid me even when a soldier held a torch to my face; the clothes heavy with pit dirt (thank God for Kit's foresight in making me leave my old doublet in the pit); all made a convincing picture and proved us to be what Archie said we were. All the same, the search they made was a thorough one, and if there had been anyone or

73

anything concealed, it would have been dug out by Grimston and his ferrets.

All the time the search was going on I was hard put to it to look unconcerned, to keep my face blank and stupid as befitted the account Archie had given of me; for I was terrified that I might be questioned, or that at any moment Harbottle Grimston would recognize me. However, at last Grimston was satisfied and ordered his men to leave us, and, after warning us that if we saw any strangers during the next few days we must, without fail, report the fact to the officer in charge at Tynemouth Castle, he departed not troubling to latch the door behind him.

We both stood motionless, staring at the part-open door; then Archie slowly went and pulled it to and then, breathing heavily, came and sat down at the table.

'Ralph, hinnie,' he said, 'that was a narrow thing.'

'Narrower than you knew, Archie,' I said. 'Yon officer was Harbottle Grimston.'

'D'you mean to say you know the man?' he cried. 'And that he knows you?'

'He does that,' I said, and I explained that Harbottle Grimston was one of the two officers of Hazelrigg's quartered in my mother's house in the Close, and that moreover I had seen him at the storming of Tynemouth Castle and had been afraid that he might have seen me.

'Nay, Ralph,' said Archie, 'some folks is born lucky, and I'm thinking you're one of them. First, you don't break your silly neck when you get over the wall of the Castle. Then you get a sea-fret to help you through Tynemouth, and when you do walk into a patrol, you shake it off again. Then of all the crazy things, you crawl into an adit and have the luck to crawl into a pack of bigger fools than you are, who haven't sense enough to give you up. And now, to cap all, the officer who searches this place is the very man who could recognize you and you have the monstrous good luck to be still in your pit dirt. Just supposing you'd had first go at the tub!'

He threw back his head and let out a great shout of laughter in which I did not join. The strain of the last few minutes had left me nearer tears, especially as I was by no means sure that the danger was past, and was expecting the door to burst open again and Harbottle Grimston to return at any moment. Archie saw my sober face and stopped laughing.

'Aye, lad, I know it's no laughing matter, but crying'll get us no place, now will it?' he said in a coaxing voice. 'So cheer up, Ralph. It's a grand thing to be born lucky. I've got a feeling in my bones that you've nowhere near used up all your luck yet, and some of it may even spill over on to Kit and me and the other lads, who haven't had much so far.'

He spoke with such conviction that I found myself more than half believing him; and felt the better for it.

Archie up-ended the bucket that had been knocked over: the dirty water had long since soaked into the floor. He gave the tub a friendly kick.

'I don't think you'll be needing this tonight,' he said. 'If the Lobsters come back, you were too tired to bother, after all their commotion, and you not being long used to the pit, like. There's nowt out of the ordinary in that. Just wipe the thick of the muck off with these.' He found me some old rags. 'Aye, you'll do now. There's plenty round here that don't bother with the tub every night.'

Together we put the room to rights again. This did not take long—there was little in it to be disturbed even by a determined search-party—and soon we were ready for our meal. Archie took two wooden bowls, and from the smaller cauldron, which must have been slowly cooking all day, he ladled out two large portions of thick barley broth. He handed me a bowl, and a clumsy wooden spoon. 'Fetch it to the fire,' he said. 'Pull up a cracket, if you like, or sit on the hearth.'

The porridge was thick and salty—no spice, no raisins, not even honey, much less the luxury of sugar—I would have turned up my nose at it at home. But now, it was hot and filling and very good. We finished off the meal with a measure of small ale, and I, at least, felt courage spreading outwards from my warm, comforted stomach. The meal and the warmth of the fire soon had me nodding. When Archie saw that I was scarcely listening to his talk, which seemed to be of the Border country, or of the mine—indeed, I could hardly tell what he was saying at times for the roaring of the waves of sleep that I seemed to be floating in—he stood up, yawning, stretching, and scratching himself.

'I'm dead felled myself, Ralph,' he said, and he banked up the fire for the night with small coal. 'Let's away to bed. We've got to be up with the cock the morrow.' He led the way up the ladder to the loft in the roof. The last thing I remember hearing that night was his voice, from a long way off, saying, 'Now remember, Ralph, if you hear anything during the night, just leave it to me.'

Just leave it to him: it was a comfortable thought. I turned on my straw pallet and fell asleep.

Up at cockcrow I was, wonderfully refreshed and almost ready to be cheerful again. Archie had been up a while, and as we ate our breakfast, which was the rest of last night's barley porridge, washed down with cold water, he told me he had already seen Kit, who by this time must be on his way to Newcastle. He had told Kit about Harbottle Grimston and Kit had sworn and said that altered things a bit, and they would have to get rid of me as soon as possible. But he had refused to make any plans until he had seen my mother. We were to go to work as usual. He would come back from Newcastle as soon as he could. With that Archie had had to be satisfied.

Archie put up our bait for the day, barley bread and, as a special treat, for 'I know you'll not be used to plain fare, Ralph,' an onion apiece, and filled the leather water-bottles. My task was to fill the large cauldron with water from the well in the yard. Archie put more barley to simmer all day in the small cauldron. He was just banking up the fire with small coals, having first taken a shovel of hot coals from it and put them into a curious iron box with holes in the sides, and a handle to it, when a thump on the door made my heart beat fast. But it was only one of the miners, who pushed the door open and put his cheerful face round it. He gave me a shy nod, and said to Archie, 'Come on, Archie hinnie, we're all ready for off.'

The sky was grey and the morning star still in the sky as we all clumped through the yard. A woman shaking a pallet outside her door gave me a curious stare, and a dog rushed out and sniffed and barked suspiciously at me. Otherwise I could have believed it was true that I had been doing this every day for the last few months. Dressed in the clothes Archie had provided— heavy boots with wooden soles, hoggers, jerkin black-bright with coal grime, hard leather cap, and with a leather bottle slung over my shoulder, I was indistinguishable from the others.

The distance between the cottages and the pit was not as great as it had seemed the previous night, scarcely ten minutes walk. When we reached the sloping field where our pit was, I found I was enough of a hostman's son to have a good look round. Our pit had obviously once been part of a much bigger venture. There were several shafts in the field and, at the bottom of the slope, a disused engine shed showed that once the workings had not relied on adits alone but had had chain and dippers also to keep them clear of water. A rambling group of huts, now neglected, suggested that this field had once been busy enough and prosperous enough to support a gang of surface workers—corvers, a smith, a stableman, and a keeker or two. Now our surface workers were two men and a tired-looking donkey. I wondered who had owned the field before the Committee of Parliament had confiscated and sold it.

But it was time to go down the pit. Now I saw why the basket of live coals had been brought. Archie approached our shaft—the rest of us standing well back—and slung the coals down it, then hastily retreated. Nothing happened.

'That's all right: no surfet the day,' said Archie. 'Come on, Cud, he said to the winder, 'let's get started.'

He climbed into the noose on the winding rope and nodded to Cud, who started the donkey on its round track and slowly Archie sank from sight. All the miners waited in silence until a signal on the rope showed that Archie had reached the bottom safely. The men told me that they took turns at being the first to descend: the presence of surfet might be detected (and disposed of) by the live coals, but there was no way of dealing with styth, which could creep up and kill a man before he had time to cry 'God's mercy'. I was learning fast about the risks in mining to life and limb, I had always known about the dangers lurking in mines but, till then, I had heard only of their effect on the money invested in the pits. Perhaps the men sensed this: they were never really at ease with me and I had a feeling that they only tolerated me because Kit had persuaded them—except, of course, Archie, who was still at heart a Borderer and divided men into only two groups, those he worked with and those he worked against.

Then it was my turn to make the descent of the shaft. It was even more terrifying than the ascent of the previous evening; then I had, at least, been returning to day; now I was swinging slowly into darkness and all the commonplace, unfamiliar dangers of the mine: styth, surfet, falls, floods, or subterranean devils which destroyed men in seconds. So I was glad when I reached the bottom, yet afraid to be there.

The day's toil began. It was an endless, back-breaking monotonous day, in hot stuffy darkness not far from hell, with only six poor candles to keep the demons away: a day which kept my hands and feet busy, but left my mind free, open to all the miseries it could dream of. Because I have not mentioned my troubles again, you must not imagine they were forgotten. I was two persons, one talking, and even joking, working, and noticing; the other, deep down within me, sick for home, and sober little Emmet, and Alyse, and my mother, and wild with fear that I should never see any of them again. And all the time the second self threatened to rise like floodwater and drown the other.

Time dragged by until at last the hewers announced that they had worked their stint for the day. I hooked the last corf of coal to the rope and watched it swing upwards to day. The hewers followed, then I ascended, and Archie came last of all. Once again it was good to breathe the fresh air and see the evening sunlight. This time there was some activity at the top. Half a dozen pack-horses were being loaded with best coal, and the riddler, who was in charge of the casual sale of coal as well as of the sorting of it, was in high spirits and joking with the drover of the horses, as he loaded the panniers. The coal was all ready waiting in the measuring vats, and when we all lent a hand the panniers were soon full. Ale appeared and went round. Then the drover gave a smart smack on the flank of the leading horse and the train started off.

'You'll never guess who that load was for,' said the riddler, smiling complacently.

'Oh, come on, man, out with it,' said one of the hewers.

'John Stobart. Aye, I thought that would make you look.'

Even I had heard of John Stobart, the biggest brewer in Shields, big enough to be a threat to the monopoly of Newcastle brewers who, try as they might, had never yet managed to catch him supplying a ship at Shields, but had sworn that when they did they would break him.

'How come he wanted our coal?' Archie wanted to know.

'Oh, never mind about that,' interrupted one of the hewers, 'did he pay in cash or promises?'

'Oh, cash, never fear. I'm not daft,' said the riddler, triumphantly waving a purse that clinked. 'And that's not all; if he likes the look of this lot, he's sending tomorrow for another load. Seems like, what with all the troubles this summer, good coal's not so easy to come by.'

'See, I told you you were lucky,' said Archie's voice at my side, and then, more loudly for them all to hear, 'It's Ralph as has brought us luck. I told you he would.'

But the other miners thought it was early to be saying that: they would wait a while longer before they felt sure of it.

'How about some of that money now?' asked one of the hewers. 'Let's go home by the "Swan".'

This proposal was well received by the others but the riddler would have none of it. 'Nay, you know the bargain,' he said. 'This goes to Kit; he's in charge of share-outs.'

There was some mild grumbling, but nothing could really pull down their spirits, and we went home together with a deal of good humour and laughter and friendly scuffling.

Before we reached Pitmen's Row we saw a woman coming towards us; even in the distance her agitation was plain to see.

'Why, that's Ellen!' cried Archie. 'What can ail her? I hope there's nowt gone wrong with Kit.'

We all hurried to Kit's wife.

'What's up, lass?' said Archie.

'Oh, Archie,' she said, 'isn't our Kit with you? I thought maybe he'd gone to the pit first. I couldn't sit at home waiting any longer. What can have happened? Oh, Archie, d'you think he's been taken? What's going to happen to us all? I told him to have nowt to do with the lad.' She gave me a savage look.

'Nay, Ellen, it's not like you to work yourself up like this. It's hardly sunset yet. It's a fair walk to Newcastle and back, especially with the roads deep in clart after all the rain. And he wasn't forced to get to see Mistress Cole the first time he tried, you know.'

She calmed down a little but muttered something about Kit having 'no call to go risking his neck for a hostman's brat'.

The miners, their spirits dampened now, were inclined to

agree with her, but Archie spoke up:

'Now fair's fair, Ellen. We don't know that his neck's in danger, yet. And any road, he's doing it for what he'll can get out of it for us and for himself, so leave the lad alone. Let's get home and you'll maybe find Kit there before you. And if he is, we've got something that'll gladden his heart.'

The riddler told the story of the new customer and they all dwelt, though with less belief than before, on the possibility that the brewer might become a regular buyer. By the time we had reached the cottages, Ellen was calm again, at least to outward appearances.

A trifling incident to remember after all these years, you think? An over-anxious woman fearful before she had cause to be. Well, yes, but it made a strong impression on me. In the tangled skein of my feelings at that time, one strong strand was guilt that I had brought so much trouble to my mother and had endangered what was left of the family fortunes. Now another strand was added—awareness that other people, even people I scarcely knew, might be in danger because of me, even though, as Archie had said, it might be hope of gain, and not love of me that had put them in danger. However, there was nothing I could do about it now. Kit had chosen his path, just as I had mine, and both of us had dragged others with us.

So we were, after all, a subdued little group that separated and went to our several cottages to wait for Kit's return. Archie, good-hearted Archie, who reminded me more every hour of Jackie (what, I wondered, had happened to Jackie?) tried to cheer me up, telling me to take no notice of Ellen.

'She's just a woman, Ralph lad. They always want to play safe. "Better safe than sore"—that's their motto. But that never got anybody any place. Anyway, she's fair daft about Kit and can hardly bear him out of her sight. Don't know how he can stick it, myself. She should have had half a dozen bairns to keep her busy. You'll see, the minute he's back, anything he says'll be all right with Ellen—even looking after a hostman's brat.'

He kept up a cheerful flow of talk, and all the time he talked we were getting out the tub and the hot water, and the pattern of the previous night was repeated. And again I began to feel that I was what I was pretending to be, and that the Close and the people in it were just a dream.

Archie was in the tub removing as much of the day's grime as he could when Kit called, 'Anybody home?' and pushed the door open. There were no bolted doors and no formalities in Pitmen's Row. I was bursting to ask what had happened but suddenly found myself tongue-tied.

'So you got back all right,' said Archie. 'What happened, Kit? Did you get into Newcastle? Did you get to see Mistress Cole? Did she agree? What did she say? Hold on a minute till I'm out of this.' With a heave that sent the water cascading over the side, he was out of the tub and drying himself in front of the fire. I waited anxiously to hear what Kit had to say, trying to read his expression in the flickering of the flames.

'Aye, I got into Newcastle all right; and what's more I got out again,' he said drily. 'And I did get to see Mistress Cole—in her own good time, mind you: too busy she was at first. That's a fine watchdog she's got, Ralph. What's his name? Trumbell. Couldn't see what I could have to say that would interest Mistress Cole.'

So Trumbell was still with her. I was suddenly glad of Thomas Trumbell.

And how had Kit persuaded Thomas Trumbell to let him talk to my mother? He did not tell Archie, just smiled faintly and said, 'Never mind how: she *did* listen.'

I found my tongue at last. 'Kit, what did she say when you told her about me? What did she do?'

A spurt of flame from the coals showed his face: it was wearing, for a moment, a softer expression.

'Why, what should she do, Ralph, and her having the one son and him lost?' Kit paused. . . . 'She burst into tears.'

I had expected anything but that, and on the instant, to my utter horror, I did that very thing myself.

Nor could I stop. All my fear of the future, all my regret for my folly, welled up in great ugly sobs. There was silence except for my sobbing and a sudden sputtering of the coals. Then Archie cleared his throat and said awkwardly, 'Come on, you great gowk, Ralph. You don't know whether there's owt to cry about yet. Here you are.' He thrust a rag into my hand. 'Fine sight you look; proper magpie you are.'

'Nay, let him have his cry out. He's nowt but a bairn away from home, when all's said and done.'

This sympathy—from Kit, of all people—did not, strangely

enough, make me give way still further, but actually helped me to check my sobs. Archie's kindness I could accept: I wanted no pity from Kit.

'I'm all right,' I said. 'I won't do that again. Tell us what happened, Kit, please.'

'Well, your mother had been nearly distracted, not knowing whether you were alive or dead. She knew you had followed George Selby to Tynemouth. Trumbell, as you thought, had seen you go, and had even, as you didn't know, torn some way after you to try and fetch you back. When he had to give that up he went straight back to Newcastle. And all the way up the river he was wondering how to tell his news to your mother. She took it very well, apparently. Your uncle was brought into the discussion at some point, and they talked for long enough, trying to decide what to do. And all that came out of the talk was that they decided there was only one thing they could do.' Again Kit paused: I swear he got some kind of satisfaction out of keeping me in suspense.

'And that was just to wait and see what happened,' he went on. 'After all, if Newcastle turned over to the King, and if the new war defeated the King's enemies, well then you would be safe enough. In fact, Ralph, lad, I wouldn't be surprised if it had crossed the mind of Master Trumbell that, in that case, you might even turn out to be an asset to the family. Nay, you've no need to look like that; folks have to look all ways round a thing these days and Thomas Trumbell's likely to be a good friend to you yet.

'So they waited. Your mother waited at home, and Thomas Trumbell went about Newcastle to see what he could find out. Soon it was plain that Hazelrigg had the city under control, and there was no chance of *his* turning coat. And though Thomas Trumbell is a man of peace even he had not far to go before he could tell that not only was the Parliament army on the watch for trouble in the city, but was also making preparations for sending a force down the river to Tynemouth. So he went back to your house in the Close to be with your mother. During his absence there had been a moment's panic when there had been a great knocking on the door. It was a soldier from the Castle summoning Harbottle Grimston and Sydrach Simpson back to duty. The ground floor of the house had been shuttered and bolted and barred in case fighting broke out. From the

Great Chamber upstairs they had been able to see enough to guess that no time was going to be wasted before Hazelrigg's intention of attacking Tynemouth Castle was carried out. They said that even supplies of tree branches were carted down to the Quayside, so that Hazelrigg's men could fill the moat straight away, without having to search for bushes in the neighbourhood of the Castle.

'So they waited all that day, and that night. Nobody went to bed that night, Ralph.'

'Not even Emmet?' I cried incredulously.

'If Emmet is your pretty little sister, no, not even Emmet,' said Kit.

Emmet not sent to bed: more than anything yet this gave me some measure of my mother's anxiety.

'Well, early next day,' Kit went on, 'the news was brought up the river that Tynemouth had fallen, that Lilburne was dead, and his men either killed or captured. I don't think anyone was surprised, except, maybe, that it had happened so quickly.'

'What did they decide to do then?' Archie asked the question for me.

'Thomas Trumbell decided to go to Hazelrigg himself and ask for mercy for you, always supposing you were still alive. After all, you were nowt but a silly lad with a head filled with nonsense by a father who paid the price for his own folly four years ago.'

There was hardly time to resent the way he referred to my father before Kit went on:

'So Trumbell went to Hazelrigg's headquarters and after a long weary wait, was, because he is known as a supporter of Parliament, allowed some minutes of the great man's time. Hazelrigg could give him no news of you, of course, but he did, as a great favour, give Master Trumbell permission to go to Tynemouth and try to find out whether you were a prisoner, or among the dead. But that was the only concession he would make, even to Trumbell. If you were a prisoner, you would receive the same treatment as the rest. Parliament was determined to have no more trouble and would show mercy to none. If it had followed this policy during the first war, there would never have been a second war. So there you are, Ralph. You know what to expect.'

He paused. I knew he had something unpleasant still to tell. 'Oh, yes; another thing. Master Trumbell said that from talk he heard at headquarters it's pretty certain they're going to have a go at searching the mines for escaped Royalists.'

My spirits could scarcely have been lower.

'How about a drink, Archie,' he said. 'It's dry work talking.' Curse the man, how could he sit there sounding so cheerful?

Archie found three leather mugs and poured us all a draught of the thin ale. 'Come on, hurry up, Kit; don't torment the lad: he doesn't need telling he's in trouble.'

'All right; all right, Archie. Give a man time to tell a tale his own way. He can have the worst first and get it over with quickly.' Kit took a long draught of the ale and nursed the mug in his hands for the rest of his story. 'Now, where was I? Oh, yes. Well, Master Trumbell went straight back to the Close to give Mistress Cole an account of his meeting with Hazelrigg. They couldn't help wondering if they would have done better to have stayed away from Hazelrigg. They might have waited until your uncle sailed and then given out that you had gone with him—got rid of until you simmered down, because you had taken the news of your mother's approaching marriage so badly. This had been one of the ideas they had thought of, but it was too late for that now. So as soon as he'd had a bite to eat, Master Trumbell set off for Tynemouth.

'The pass he had, signed by Hazelrigg himself, won him from Major Cobham a sight of the muster rolls which had been taken into safe-keeping by Cobham. It didn't take him long to find out that you had indeed been in the Castle—not that he'd had much doubt about it. He was allowed to see some of the bodies of the King's men—not all, for a number of them had already been shovelled into pits without overmuch ceremony: there's some poor souls will never know where their men or their sons lie. But you were not among those he did see. I think he half hoped you would be: it would have been easier in the long run. Nor were you among the prisoners.

'So all the news he could take back to your mother, Ralph, was that if you were not lying unidentified in a common grave outside the Castle walls, you must be in hiding somewhere. Just about the time you were climbing up the Short Sands cliffs, Thomas Trumbell must have been on his way back up the river wondering how best to tell your mother that her only son might be dead, or might be alive: all that could be said for certain was that you were not a prisoner—yet.

'Your mother heard his news more calmly than he had feared: at least she felt she could still hope. She had news of her own to tell Trumbell. The house had already been searched by Parliament troops to see if you had managed to get home. You *were* a fool to put your own name on that roll, Ralph. Mind you, any house with Royalist connexions was bound to be searched sooner or later. Captain Simpson it was that conducted the search.'

Captain Simpson. Who in the name of goodness was Captain Simpson? Of course, the other officer billeted at our house in the Close.

'It appears that he was as kind as his uniform would let him be, but he had to warn your mother that she must expect other visits at any time of the day or night. Worst of all, he told her that his lieutenant, Harbottle Grimston, the officer who was here last night I gather, was one of those in charge of the search for escaped Royalists, and would not be returning to his billet for the next few days—maybe not for some time.'

So the search was to go on, and one of the officers in charge of it was one of the few Parliament men who knew my face. What if he searched Archie's cottage again? I turned my attention back to what the others were saying. Their thoughts had been following similar lines to mine.

'It's hard to tell one lad from another in their pit dirt,' Archie was saying, 'but the lad can't stay black all the time. I've been wondering about Sunday: it'd look queer if he wasn't clean then.' Then for a moment his face brightened. 'Mebbe they're too holy to search on Sunday. Yes, I wouldn't mind betting they are.'

At any other time it might have been funny—Archie worrying about whether it would be safe for me to have a clean face on Sunday. Though there was something about Kit Sanderson that made me ill at ease with him, I had to speak now. 'But, Kit,' I said, 'you still haven't told us whether you all decided on anything or not.'

'No more I haven't,' said Kit. 'Well, your mother, or rather Master Trumbell, agreed, no argument about it at all, to take all our coals for the sea trade and give us the full hostmen's price.' Curse him and his coals, why didn't he get on with his story? 'And we've agreed that you're to keep out of sight and harm's way until St. Luke's Fair.'

Till St. Luke's! But that was more than two months off. How could I stay here until then? And anyway, why St. Luke's?

'We are going to get you back into Newcastle at St. Luke's, when it's full of folk. After that, it'll be up to your mother and Master Trumbell to get you on to a collier going to the Continent, where you'll stay with your uncle until the troubles are all over. There now, how does that strike you?' And he emptied his pot of ale with an air of complete satisfaction.

He was obviously so pleased with his scheme and so full of confidence that for a moment I felt myself catching some of it from him. Yet hope was struggling with a dawning realization that my exile from home was going to be long. The troubles, as Kit called them, had been dragging on, in one way or another for almost ten years—most of that part of my life that I could remember: it was hard for me to imagine that a day might come when they might be ended. And there were things I had to know. Archie was asking my questions for me.

'Hold on a minute, Kit,' he said. 'Sounds easy the way you say it, but just *how* are we going to keep the lad out of harm's way until St. Luke's? You've just told us that the Parliament men are determined to round up every last King's man this time. One of the officers in charge of the search just happens to know Ralph by sight. You've said it's more than likely the coal pits'll be well searched. And anyway, it'll be a wonder if it's not let slip sooner or later that my brother, so-called, hasn't been here since spring at all but turned up about the time of the bother over at the Castle. Then we'll all be nicely in the cart. Nay, Kit, I'm a hanged man if I can make out what you're so cheerful about, and I have my doubts whether Ralph here can either, from the look on his face.'

'D'you think we didn't think of all that, me and the lad's mother? And Thomas Trumbell thought of a few more snags, too. I never met any other body as good as him at that: he's a useful man, Ralph. The whole thing was given a good going over, I can tell you.'

'Oh, come on, Kit,' said Archie reproachfully, 'you know you've got something worked out.'

'All right. All right. Now, listen, the pair of you. It so

happened that this morning, just before I went to the Close, I dropped in at the "White Hart" in the Bigge Market for a drop to get my nerve up to tackle Mistress Cole. I'm not used to fine folk, Ralph, you know.'

Kit nervous? I could hardly believe it as he sat there radiating self-confidence.

'Well, who should be sitting in the chimney corner but Old Adam?'

'Adam! You mean...' But Kit did not give Archie a chance to finish. He frowned at him and said, with some underlying meaning I could not understand, 'Yes, the travelling doctor.'

But Archie seemed startled and would not be silent. 'Why, he must be crazy to come to the Fair. This summer, I mean.'

Kit was still frowning at Archie. It was difficult to see in the flickering firelight, but did he shake his head slightly, and give a warning glance at me? I barely noticed it at the time, but later, when my suspicions were awakening, I was almost certain that my mind had stored away an impression that he did.

'Well, that was what *I* thought, as well,' Kit was hurrying on, 'but Adam said that there were some spices he needed that he could only get at the Fair.'

'But even in an ordinary year he usually gets away on his round before the end of the Lammas Fair.' Archie's voice still held surprise in it.

'I know that as well as you do, Archie. For Heaven's sake, let's get on with my tale, or we'll be here half the night.' Again I stored in my mind a half-formed impression that there was something more than ordinary impatience in Kit's voice. Anyway, there were no more interruptions of Archie's making.

'Well, it seems that he's not been feeling over grand lately—been in bed with a fever. He certainly did look poorly, but he's not as young as he was, of course. But he thought he'd be all right again once he got into the good Northumbrian air; especially if he could get a bit of help for this round as he sometimes has before. He was looking for a lad to take with him, but likely lads weren't easy to come by. Most of them were frightened to go with him round Northumberland just now: it was too dangerous now the war had started up again. Not that Adam was for blaming them—never heard him blame anybody in his life.

'Aye, I can see from your face, Ralph, that you've guessed it.

This is where you come in. I told Adam that we had in the pit a lad from Elsdon, who would be going back there for the winter anyway, and seeing as it had been a poor year for selling our coal, we'd none of us say owt if he left earlier than we had bargained for. I told him, Ralph, that you'd be glad of a chance to earn your food and a shilling or two by going with him as far as Elsdon. He was willing to take you on the character I gave you. He just wants a look at you tonight, but it's as good as settled.

'So you see, when I did get to Mistress Cole, I had a plan all ready. She didn't take much persuading to it. Nor did Master Trumbell. Not that they liked it overmuch, but, risky though it may be, they could see that it isn't nearly as risky as leaving you here. So there you are, Ralph, as from first thing tomorrow you are boy to Old Adam. I had arranged to meet him again this afternoon and fetch him here. He's in our house now: Ellen's fixing him a meal. You might as well come and let him have a look at you now.'

Kit was pleased with himself. He could hardly be said to be smiling (I don't think he smiled very much) but the lines of his face were a little less grim.

'And, Ralph,' he said, 'leave the talking to Archie and me. Just answer his questions—no more.'

But I was not as pleased with the scheme as Kit, and apparently Archie too, seemed to be.

'What's the good of getting to Elsdon? I thought you said my mother would try to get me on to a collier leaving the Tyne at the time of St. Luke's Fair?' I asked.

'Now, Ralph, there's always been ways from the Marches to Newcastle even at the worst of times. The Elsdon folk'll fix it for you. We'll see that they get to hear about you. So come on, let Adam have a look at you. And remember, the story's the same as before—you're from Elsdon, you're Ralph Reede, Archie's brother; this is your first summer in the pit. Archie, you'd better come with us. After all, he's not very bright in the head, and he *is* your little brother.'

Kit almost making a joke! He *must* be pleased with his scheme. Yet, although by now I felt I was living in a dream the course of which nothing I could do would change, I had to make a last protest.

'But, Kit,' I said, 'I don't know a thing about Elsdon, or

Archie's folks. Wouldn't it be better to tell the man the truth? I'm bound to give myself away to him sooner or later.'

'There's enough folks in this already, Ralph,' Kit said. 'And if Old Adam has no notion that you're other than we say you are, it'll be better for him if things do go wrong—and they'll be less likely to go wrong. You've got this night to find out as much as you can from Archie here. And anyway, I've told Adam that you're so shy and backward from living all your life in the Wilds of Wanie that you scarcely ever open your mouth in front of strangers. In fact, Ralph,' he said with a sly look, 'he knows that you're not over-bright, though a good, obedient lad that can be counted on to do exactly as he's told, but no more. Nay, stop fashing yourself, lad. Adam's a kind old man, and if he wants to get through his Northumberland round before winter, he's got to get started pretty soon, so he's not going to be over fussy about you.'

It turned out as Kit had prophesied, and when I did at last get to bed that night it was a long time before I fell asleep, for round my head danced a motley crowd of thoughts—of Elsdon and of the Close; of Archie's mother and young brother; of my mother and Emmet; of Alyse and Thomas Trumbell; of the glitter of coal and of the glitter of the coins that Kit had brought to me from my mother, and that Archie and I had clumsily stitched into the band of my breeches and the hem of my old buff jerkin. But, gradually, relief that my mother knew where I was and what I was going to do steadied my whirling thoughts and at last I fell asleep.

Chapter 10

Early next morning, so early that dawn was scarcely a grey gleam in the east, I said good-bye to Archie, who had come to the end of the yard to see me go. In the short time I had known him, the man from the Marches had been so kind to me, and what was perhaps even more important then, so sure I was lucky, so confident that nothing could go wrong with Kit's plans, that when I waved the last time and saw him turn to go back to the cottage, it was almost as if it were truly a brother I was parting from, and I felt forlorn indeed.

'Don't fret, lad,' said Old Adam, 'you'll find I'm not a hard master if you listen to what I say and do as you're bid. And it'll not be so very long before you see the rest of your folks again.'

He was trying to be kind, but I was vexed that my face was so easy to read. Archie and Kit had warned me about this and here I was giving away my feelings again. There and then I vowed to school myself to show the world a blank face henceforth, and I think I succeeded pretty well. I mumbled, 'Yes, Master Adam,' in reply, and took up the leading rein to guide the pack-donkey over the rough track.

'There's no need to do that, Ralph,' said Adam. 'Jennie knows the way as well as her master, don't you, lass?' He gave her a friendly smack and she turned round her head in appreciation.

Jennie was as laden as any animal could be: on each side was a pannier full of Adam's herbs and salves and potions, and various packages in tarred cloth were attached to leather bands which seemed to be dangling all round her, to say nothing of two sooty pans and a large drum which bounced gaily whenever she went faster than the mildest pace. She did not seem to mind, however, but ambled along at a gentle pace which matched admirably Adam's steady stride. Old Adam they had called him and to a lad who at fifteen thought anyone more than twenty almost a dotard, he seemed old indeed. His beard, in startling contrast to his bronzed skin, was white, and he had bushy white eyebrows which, in determined fashion, went their own way. Yet his face, though lined, was firm-fleshed, and the bright blue of his eye was still unfaded. Kit had said that Adam was just recovering from a fever, yet he seemed hale enough. His step might seem unhurried but I discovered that first day that, bred in a town as I had been, it was all I could do to keep up with him for hours on end.

He caught me staring at him and the lines round his eyes deepened for a moment but he said nothing as I hastily moved my gaze back to Jennie.

'Let's put your pack on Jennie's back, Ralph: she won't mind,' he said.

Then he took my little bundle (a shirt and stockings given to me by Archie) and somehow found a place for it on Jennie's back.

And my wanderings through Northumberland began.

Strangely, though I know that fears and anxieties, rising at times near to terror, were uppermost in my mind, when I look back on those weeks with Adam, it is the patches of peace I remember first. Old Adam loved to talk but he never expected me to answer him, and his eyes never missed the cluster of late harebells trembling where all else was still, or the spray of pale honeysuckle almost lost in a tangled hedgerow. He showed me the infinite variety of growing things that men in towns have forgotten how to use. He found food for us that late summer and autumn, when Scots and English, Cavaliers and Roundheads, had crawled like hungry caterpillars across unhappy Northumberland and stripped it bare. He found us leaves and roots; berries gay and showy; mushrooms hiding under rotten wood and leaves. Most of all he had a store of information about the medicines that could be made from plants. God had sent us, he said, a cure for every fleshly ill, if foolish men but knew where to find it. On our way from village to village we gathered plants for his medicines: coltsfoot roots from the hedgerows; late wild strawberries hiding neat and bright beneath their leaves and crying out to be eaten, but too precious for that; tansy flaunting brazenly everywhere; rough comfrey making ditches gay; and yellow fleabane in the marshes; even dull nettles.

One day we climbed down the rocks to a lonely little bay not far from St. Mary's island, and with the boys and girls of Hartley, I paddled in the pools and collected a particular seaweed which Adam wanted for one of his lotions.

There was a kind of grub we used to collect and put to dry on large stones which had been heated in a fire. When they were dried, we used to powder them by pounding them with another stone which had been heated and then allowed to get cool again. This powder was much sought after by timid sufferers from toothache, for if it was put regularly into a hollow tooth, the tooth would drop out.

Adam made no secret of his medicines. He told the villagers how they were made and encouraged them to try to make them themselves, though not often successfully: they thought that potions made by his hands must somehow be different. He had a special stock of simples made from herbs which had grown in the shadow of the Picts' Wall.*

'They're no different from other plants, Ralph,' Old Adam assured me, 'but if it helps sick folk to think they are, well, it can't do any harm and might do good.'

Adam was always willing to let me watch and, later, to help in the preparation of his medicines. The only other doctor I had known was the one who had cared for the Cole family as long as I could remember—fat old Master Tyzacke, in the Side, Newcastle's leading physician who was far too important to visit his patients but sent his assistant to bring him an account of their symptoms. *His* services were too costly for any but the Coles, the Riddells, the Milbankes, the Carrs and the other merchant families of the city. Adam would never be rich: his services were paid for only occasionally with money, commonly with barley bread, or some eggs or cheese, and not seldom only with thankful words or looks.

None of this was known to me, of course, that quiet Sunday dawn when I left Archie's home only five mornings after I had left my own home in the Close. Five mornings before, I had been a turmoil of anger and resentment: now I was scarcely calmer but my emotions were very different. All lesser feelings were submerged in a vast fear of being taken by the Roundheads and condemned not to death certainly, but to a death in life in the plantations of the Indies or the galleys of the Vene-

* The Picts' Wall was the name always given to the Roman Wall which ran from Wallsend to Carlisle.

tians. It would be pleasant to believe that mingled with my selfish fear, there was some gratitude for those who had helped me or some guilt that Adam might, unwittingly, be in some danger because of me, but I cannot really think that it was so: after all I was only fifteen. My fear had to remain shut up inside me, since Adam did not know my real reason for coming with him, so I tried to concentrate on what he was saying but most of his talk flowed over me for, no matter how much I told myself it would serve no purpose, my whole body seemed to be watching and listening for the troop of Parliament soldiers which could appear and make me prisoner. At every turn of the lane which was leading us to Chirton, I expected to find Harbottle Grimston straddling the way.

Yet the countryside was peaceful enough: as peaceful as I could ever remember having seen it. The first part of our journey lay through scenes that had been familiar to me all my life: areas of mine workings where barley and oats, pale from lack of sun and staggering from the lash of that rainy summer, grew right to the edge of fields where the crop that grew was of sheds and shafts and heaps of unsold coal.

Chirton was still asleep as we passed through. I durst not ask Adam if we were going through Tynemouth village, but not long after Chirton the lane forked: we took the left fork and I knew I was to be spared the nightmare of coming close to the Castle again. All the time now we were getting farther away from Tynemouth and the sun was rising higher and higher. My spirits seemed to rise with it. The sky was blue and the great fleecy clouds scarcely moved and presently on our right we saw the sea. By now I could even spare a thought for poor Emmet who liked the sea so much and was still shut up in the noisy city.

As we walked across the fields and drew near to the cluster of fishermen's cottages that Adam said was the village of Cullercoats, the scene was so peaceful that I almost dared to hope that I might forget my fear for a while. Yet I knew that if I stood at the end of the headland where the nets lay drying in the sun and looked south across the curve of brown sand that ended in a rocky headland, I might make out on yet another headland that repeated the first one, the outline of Tynemouth Castle. We only *seemed* to have left it far behind.

Before very long Adam and I were being taken into one of the

Cullercoats cottages and invited to share the family meal. The cottage was small and dark like Archie's and it was crowded by the time we were all inside: the Dagg family, mother and daughter, father and three grown sons, and Adam and I. When we had all found a place at the table and received our bowls of fish and turnips, I picked up my big bone spoon to begin, and then blushed for shame, because Mistress Dagg had turned to Adam, and all fell silent, as he asked a blessing on the food we were to eat. The daughter of the house noticed my embarrassment and did her best, kind soul, to put me at my ease. But as all she, not knowing me, could do was to ask well-intentioned but unwelcome questions about myself, I answered her so briefly that she thought me churlish and left me alone.

The talk round the table was of the sort that you would hear anywhere, at any time, when old friends meet after a while: of deaths, and births, and courtships, and how the fishing had been, and the wet summer that promised a bad harvest. It was likely to be a hard winter for poor folks, they said; harder even than '44 when the Scots had eaten the country bare. And who could see where it would all end? The Daggs told Adam that Cullercoats had been raided for supplies by Lilburne's men on the day he turned over to the King. 'Precious little there was to take, Adam. We'd seen to that.' Then the following day their cottages and sheds had been searched for fugitives by Hazelrigg's men: a great, ugly brute of a man had been in charge, they said.

Before the meal was over the first patient had poked his head through the open doorway. Our hostess in no uncertain terms called out to him to come back later when 'the poor man had had his bite in peace', but Adam intervened, and told the youth to wait, and hurried through his meal in spite of Mistress Dagg's urgings that he should take his time. I was sent to bring in the big pack. Jennie was peacefully cropping the grass and sea pinks and lady's fingers above the little bay and scarcely raised her head as I unfastened the pack.

When I reached the cottage again, the menfolk were leaving it. Inside, the women had cleared away the bowls and spoons, and while the daughter took them outside to wash, the mother was filling a wooden bucket with hot water from the cauldron, and standing it at one end of the trestle table which had been moved nearer the door where the light was better for Adam to work by. I undid the large pack and Adam spread out on the table the containers with their salves and ointments, and pastes and lotions and powders. This was my first day. Later, when I knew what each container held, I used to make all the preparations and hand Adam whatever he asked for while he worked. Mistress Dagg—Adam granted all the women we met the courtesy of that title, fisherman's wife or laird's lady—laid out a pile of clean rags; Adam spread out his tools—razor, scissors, pincers, knives—and we were ready for the first patient, the youth who had precipitated these preparations.

The afternoon sped past, and I scarcely noticed its going, so interesting was it to watch Adam at work, and see the faith the patients had in him, and the hope with which they took away his simples. Mistress Dagg helped him: she was clearly used to his ways and had some skill herself, and Adam usually left her to put the bandages on sores he had cut and cleaned. I did whatever I could, and listened to everything Adam said.

When the last patient had gone, I was surprised and infinitely pleased to hear Adam say, 'You shape well, Ralph lad. Doesn't he, Mistress Dagg?'

'He does that,' she replied. 'A deal better than that last lad you had. You're well shot of him: in too much of a hurry to be done, he was. What did you say you did before Adam took you on?'

My pleasure in the praise rapidly changed to consternation when I saw that her interest in me had been aroused, but I had only just mumbled that I had been 'down the pits' when her husband and sons came back from their banishment and her attention was distracted from me. Then Adam told me to go outside with him for a breath of fresh air, and I was surprised how sweet and clean it seemed after the smell of sickness that had been in my nostrils all afternoon.

Adam led us out of the village and towards the cliff tops above the little harbour, and then down a rough path on to the sand below, where several boys and young men were playing football with a clout ball, watched by a group of admiring girls and harried by two excited mongrels. As we approached, the lively group grew gradually still as first the dogs, then the girls and finally the footballers noticed us. Adam knew them all by name and they smiled, rather shyly, when he spoke to them. To my embarrassment he told them that he had brought his lad,

Ralph Reede—he smiled at me—to join in the game. They made a place for me willingly enough, but self-consciousness had descended on their game and it was not long before a boy suggested it was growing too dark to play and the rest agreed. Adam, resting on a near-by rock, called out that he was going to stay out a little while longer and asked a boy to take me back to the Daggs' cottage, and we all straggled back up the cliff path and through the village. With obvious relief, the lad delivered me to the Daggs' doorway, called out, 'Here's Ralph Reede back,' murmured something about seeing me later, and left me.

It was the daughter's voice that called out, 'Well, come on in, Ralph Reede. What're you waiting for?' (Even at the end of my journeyings with Adam, I found it difficult to walk into a house without a by-your-leave, though I had soon learnt that this was expected: only a complete stranger knocked and waited to be asked in.) I went into the cottage and was surprised to find that the girl—I think her name was Mary Ann—was the only one at home. However, she gave no explanation but bustled hospitably round me in a manner just like her mother's that made me homesick, for it made me think of Emmet trying to be like my mother, and in no time at all was ladling out a steaming bowl of fish, which she handed to me.

'What about waiting for Adam?' I asked.

'Oh, the others'll be a while yet,' she said. 'We're not to wait for them,' and she ladled out another bowl of fish for herself.

The fish broth with lumps of fish and a good sprinkling of shrimps was very tasty. I hoped she would offer me a second helping. She did, piling my bowl high. For all her grown-up ways she must have been as shy as I was because she said no more until we had both finished our broth.

'You'll be wanting your bed,' she said at last. 'Come on, then.'

'What about Jennie?' I asked.

'Jennie's been taken care of, no thanks to you. You're a bit late thinking about the poor beast, aren't you? Adam's far too soft with his lads. Everybody says that.'

I was vexed, both with myself for having forgotten Jenny, and with her for speaking to me so, but I said nothing. I was not going to argue with a strange girl: the less I said to anyone the better. Ralph Reede was already a little wiser than Ralph

96

Cole would have been.

'All right, there's no need to sulk,' said Mary Ann. 'Come on, give us a hand with this.'

She was opening one of the two heavy oak chests and lifting out its contents: a few worn garments, some yarn for making nets, and old carved wooden cradle. The kist was soon empty. By some manipulation, however, she moved a section of its wooden floor. Part of the earth floor under the chest had been hollowed out, and a deep recess, lined with tarred cloth, had been made. In it were the Daggs' few treasures. It was too dark for me to see what they were, but one was the worn woollen blanket which Mary Ann pulled out and handed over to me.

'There you are,' she said. 'That's one thing the Scots didn't get, nor the Castle men, neither.'

A feeling of shame came over me that people could be so poor that an old blanket was hidden away as carefully as my mother had hidden, since 1644, the Cole silver plate and her remaining jewels and gold coin; and that I had ever listened to and shared all the indignation of the still fat Newcastle merchants who visited at the house in the Close and ranted at the way they had been plundered by Scots and Parliament. The three gold coins that my mother had sent to me by way of Kit, to be used in an emergency, seemed to burn into my side. Neither Kit nor Archie had made any comment on them. As I looked at the old worn blanket, it came to me that these fisherfolk had probably never had so much money in all their lives; nor had Kit or Archie. Yet I would have staked my life that it had never crossed the mind of either of them to keep back even one of the coins.

'What are you staring at?' There was a note of suspicion in Mary Ann's question.

'Nothing, nothing,' I said.

'Well, you can pick it up and off with it then,' she said sharply. 'Oh dear, I shouldn't have let you see that, even if Adam did say you were all right.'

'Don't worry, I won't tell anybody. Anyway, who is there to tell?'

'That's true enough,' she said, but she still looked at me suspiciously. 'Well, let's hurry up; we've kept folks out of their beds long enough.'

Then she told me that I was to sleep next door at the Sotherans'—the lad who had brought me back was Will Sotheran—as the Daggs' cottage was already crowded.

'Is Adam coming to the Sotherans'?' I asked.

'No, he's sleeping in the loft with our lads,' she said, 'but there's not room for you as well, and Jane Sotheran's only got herself and Will.'

So we went to the neighbouring cottage and Mistress Sotheran was waiting for me and made me welcome. She told Will to light a rush to show me where I was to sleep, and I was already climbing the ladder to the loft in the rafters when Mary Ann called good night.

Another strange bed. I could almost hear Alyse chiding me, 'A body can't get rested changing beds so often,' though why she was so sure about that I could not imagine for, to the best of my knowledge, she had not spent a night away from the house in the Close for the last twenty years. But I was so tired after my strange day that the clean pallet looked very inviting and I had scarcely wrapped myself in the blanket Mary Ann had lent me before I was asleep.

Once during the night I half awoke and thought I heard voices outside in the street, but when I listened only Will's gentle snore disturbed the stillness, so I turned over on to my other side, brushed a tickling straw from my face and slept once more.

Chapter 11

Adam and I broke out fast at daybreak next morning with some barley broth and water at the Daggs' and were soon on our way to the next village. That morning began my education as a doctor for Adam talked chiefly about the sick people he had seen the previous day and explained the treatment he had given to each one, for he saw I was interested. In no time at all we had reached Whitley, our next halting place. Here the day was spent in much the same way as the previous one had been.

Indeed, the pattern of our days repeated itself most of the time I was with Adam. We always set off very early and usually arrived in the next village in the late morning or early afternoon. Sometimes, if we were busy collecting herbs, or if the villages were farther apart, we might take two days to reach the next hamlet, and I learnt to sleep in the open and make myself snug under a hedge or in the shelter of a rock. At the village where we stopped, there was always a capable woman who knew Adam's ways to help him. In the evening Adam always took me to join the young men and boys, though I never learnt how to overcome my awkwardness or their shyness and would rather have stayed with Adam but never liked to tell him so. Adam always disappeared—to talk to friends of his own age, I presumed.

The days slipped by and the villages threaded themselves like beads on the string of our journey: Cullercoats, Whitley, Monkseaton, Hartley, Seaton, Seaton Delaval, Blyth. Blyth was the biggest place we had visited so far and Adam said we should stay there two days, possibly three. At home in the Close, I had heard Blyth spoken of as a port that Newcastle hostmen must watch carefully since there was a move on foot among coal-owners who were not freemen of Newcastle to develop the export of coal from there. So I looked at it with special interest but, as I remembered the busy wagon-ways and staithes of the Tyne, it was obvious that Blyth would never be more than a large village and the coal-pits round it could never be a serious challenge to the Tyne pits.

On our last afternoon in Blyth we were on our way home from visiting a bedridden old man when we were startled by the sound of a heavy explosion followed by two lighter ones. Adam knew at once what had happened. He stopped dead for a moment.

'That's an explosion in one of the pits,' he said, more to himself than to me. 'Surfet, without a doubt. God help the poor souls down there.' He said it as if it were truly a prayer. 'If there's any man left alive down the pit, there'll be work for us both. Come on, Ralph, hurry.'

He set off at a run towards the row of cottages where we were staying. Already people were streaming towards the workings, mostly women for it was working hours. When we went into the cottage that was our headquarters, the woman of the house had already made a bundle of Adam's tools and salves, and was gathering a stack of clean rags.

'Good,' said Adam. He took up the bundle of cloths and handed it to me. 'Take it, Ralph. You go ahead: don't wait for me: there's something else I want to get.'

'It's in already: I hope I did right,' said the woman of the house. 'I thought you'd be needing it.'

'You did right,' said Adam, and he took the bundle of instruments and medicines. 'Hurry, Ralph!'

There was no need to ask where the accident was: we just followed the hurrying women. When we reached the workings, it was obvious at a glance that the accident was a serious one. The whole of the top of a fair-sized shaft had been blown away, winding gear and all: only a gaping hole remained; several feet away the body of a horse lay in its own blood and entrails, through which bloated blue flies were already crawling. Near the gaping shaft men were busy at work, trying to improvise new winding gear. Until they had erected new gear over the shaft, there was nothing anybody else could do but wait. The waiting crowd was very quiet and still: I could hear the grunts of the men working.

'Why don't they have spare winding gear already cut?' I asked Adam, keeping my voice low in the quiet crowd.

'The owners won't allow it because it might not be needed.'

'But the men down there may die if they're not brought out soon,' I said.

'Most of them will be dead already, Ralph,' he said. 'Anyway, men cost nothing to replace. Now if it were horses down there . . .'

What he said was true. I had heard often enough my mother, my uncles, and other guests talk with fear of possible blasts and drownings of their pits and of the high cost of draining and clearing mines and replacing gear and horses. They were, I suppose, mostly decent, God-fearing people, yet I could not remember that they ever gave much thought to the men killed or maimed or that they ever did anything for them or their dependants. Yet how could a coal-owner pay a man if that man was not producing coal? I imagined Uncle Ralph Cole's face if I even suggested such a thing. And how could an injured man live if he had no pay coming in? 'From his savings, of course,' I could imagine Uncle Ralph saying. But if he had none? 'Thriftless lot, miners.' I had heard that before without questioning it: now I was beginning to wonder.

A shout from the men working, a stirring in the crowd: the new windlass was ready. There was a minute's confusion. Who was to make the first descent? The crowd—it was not a very large crowd after all—consisted mainly of women. The men who had improvised the windlass ought to stay on ground to work it and in case it went wrong and needed adjustment. Adam started to move towards the shaft, but one of the men caught his sleeve and I heard him mutter in a low voice, 'No, not you, not the first. You're needed too much.' His voice dropped still lower. All I could catch was, '. . . the only one we have,' then in a louder voice, 'Let somebody else go first.' To my surprise, Adam hesitated. I had not expected him to be a coward: nor did he seem afraid.

Then I heard a voice, my voice, call out, 'I'll go,' and scarcely of my own volition I had moved forward and joined Adam. Almost at the same moment a man pushed his way out of the other side of the crowd and into the space round the shaft. He was a burly man; we looked at each other for the space of a moment. I had never seen him before, but Adam seemed to know him.

'You're a fisherman, aren't you?' he asked. The man nodded. 'Let the lad go first: he's been down a pit before.'

My courage was seeping out through my fingertips which were wet with sweat, and not easy to keep from trembling. It's all very well for you, I was thinking, you're not the one that's got to go down, though I knew he was right.

So it was agreed. I listened carefully to the instructions given me—I told them I had not been in a damaged pit before—though I knew I should never remember what the men were saying. A rag soaked in vinegar was produced and tied round my nose and mouth, half choking me. A lighted candle was thrust in my hand: I was ready. I lowered myself into a sitting position on the broken edge of the shaft: the winders each took one of the windlass cranks and turned until the creaking axle brought the noose in the rope opposite my feet. Sweat broke out all over my body. I thought I should never dare to make the forward movement over the gaping shaft necessary for me to get on to the rope. I swallowed hard, sucking at my lips. I glanced across the axle and saw Adam's steady look: I leant forward, caught the rope with my sweating hands, pulled it forward a little towards me, as Archie had shown me, hooked my right arm round it, arranged my left leg and knee in the noose and swung my body off the edge of the shaft. The rope jerked and creaked as it tightened under my weight: it swung outward because I had put my weight on it too suddenly, but my left arm was free to ward off the wall of the shaft. At last the rope steadied: the first stage was over. I nodded a signal to the winders—I durst not trust my voice—and slowly and jerkily I began the descent.

I know of no way of measuring time or space that takes account of fear. After an age I saw by the glimmering light of my candle the corf of coal that weighted the other end of the rope swing slowly past my feet, my body, my head. How deep the shaft was or how long it was before my feet felt the ground I cannot say. I gave the signal on the rope that would tell the winders that I had reached the bottom alive. I heard a faint cheer and looked up: I could see nothing but that tiny square of blessed light which miners call the day. When I looked away from it, the darkness of the pit was even deeper. I held up my candle and looked around. A full corf of coal lay there: sprawled over it, face upward, was the body of the man who had brought it there just before the blast came. But for the burns on his face he might have been lying there drunk, I thought, as my light flickered on the grotesquely flung out limbs. I bent down and tried to listen to his heart: I could hear only my own blood beating in my ears. I tried to overcome my fear: this had been a man, living, hoping, fearing, only a brief hour ago. There was probably a woman up there waiting to straighten and wash those poor limbs before committing them to the earth again in decent Christian burial. I put my hand behind his shoulders to lift him up—his head fell back and his brains spattered the glittering coal. I had seen violent death before, and not long before, but in the heat of battle. This was death in the dark, that crept silently from the depths, then killed with a sudden blast from hell itself. Only the devil himself could strike down an innocent man as he went about his harmless business of getting his daily bread in the only way he could. It came to me that maybe the Auld Lad was still hiding there, waiting to strike me down next. A cold drop of sweat trickled down my forehead. I crouched there, staring at the dead man, as little able to move as he. Then the creak of the windlass penetrated my brain: someone else was coming down on the rope. I forced my back to straighten and, though my hand trembled, I raised the candle to look around. A wall of rock and coal and rubble barred the way along the main lane leading from the eye to the headways. Until it was moved, it would be impossible to know if any miners had survived. I listened: there was no sound but the slow creaking of the rope. Yet there could be men behind that barrier.

A sudden slither of rubble down the mound startled me. Then a man appeared beside me. I noticed without surprise that it was not the big fisherman nor was it Adam, but a little dark-skinned man I had never seen before.

'You can go back up now, lad,' he said. 'You've done your whack being first down. It's *my* marras that's behind there. Leave it to me and Adam; he's next down. The two of us'll manage fine.'

I shook my head. Two minutes before I had wanted nothing more than to get out of this tomb. Now nothing could have persuaded me to go. He said no more, only nodded his head. Then he took charge and under his direction I, and shortly afterwards Adam, worked with him to force a way through the mound—if way through there was.

The little man wielded a pick to break up the large pieces of rock and coal; then together, with our bare hands, we pushed the broken pieces to the side, working in silence with no breath to spare for words. He worked without haste, carefully choosing the spot for his pick to fall on. At first I wanted to urge him to greater speed, but I soon found his unhurried movements only appeared slow: I had hard work to keep up with him. Soon the sweat was crawling like lice through my hair, and down my chest, making white runnels in the coal-dust that caked my skin. Still we worked, until the whole world had shrunk into a black cavern gouged out of a glittering rock face, and the only sun left was a fitful candle.

At last the miner sat back on his heels and gestured towards the eye. 'Fetch the bottles, will you, lad?' I crawled through our cavern—it was pitiably small after all—and out to the eye, where I found the water-bottles that he or Adam must have brought. He scarcely seemed to notice when I thrust one in his hand, though he put it to his lips and tilted his head back.

'Can't keep it up much longer,' he said. So he also *had* felt the pace. 'We'll have to let the others do a shift before long.' He wiped his mouth with the back of his hand. 'Though if we don't break through soon, we'll all can knock off: there'll be no air left in there. Well, come on, don't sit there; let's get cracking again.'

After the short rest, my body was loth to start again for I had begun to feel my cuts and bruises. They were soon forgotten again, however, in the greater pain of labouring breath and straining muscles. Suddenly the miner halted.

'Stop! Listen to that a minute, lads,' he said with desperate excitement. He struck the rock ahead again. 'What do you think?'

I shook my head; I noticed Adam just tightened his lips: the heavy sound was no different to me this time from all the other times.

'Can't you hear, you great gowks?' the miner cried. 'We're nearly through. Careful now, me cannie hinnie.' Now he was talking to himself, more than to me or Adam.

The next few minutes seemed longer than all the others put together that must have dropped into the hour-glass since we had begun. Then even I could hear the different note in the thump of the pick on rock and at last we were through into a clear lane.

It was a small pit. Beyond the point where we had broken through the roof fall there were only half a dozen benches. The miners in the four benches nearest the eye had caught the worst of the explosion: their burns were terrible to see and a glance was sufficient to show that the men were dead. Only the men in the two benches farthest along the lane were still breathing. One was breathing quite strongly and did not seem to have any obvious wounds. When Adam moistened his lips with water, he stirred and muttered a little.

'He'll be all right,' said Adam. 'Get him up to day and the women'll look after him.'

As Adam went on to the next man, I heard the miner's rough voice, infinitely gentle: 'It's all right, Davie hinnie. You're all right,' and Davie's frightened muttering quietened.

The other man was in bad shape: his breath was very faint and irregular; there was a cruel gash on his forehead which had bled a great deal, and blood still trickled from the corner of his mouth. There was a great jagged piece of rock on his chest and as we lifted it away, we could feel that his ribs were broken. I started to undo Adam's bundle which he had brought down with him: among his cloths was a box, smooth from much handling. I had never seen it before and was going to open it, when Adam's hand came and took it away. Surprised, I looked at him, but he said nothing, then gave his attention to the injured man.

'Poor lad; poor lad,' he said.

Tears rushed to my eyes and a sob choked me.

Adam, without looking away from the wounded man, said, 'There's nothing here for you to do, Ralph. Go and help with the other one. You've been a good lad, Ralph Reede.'

He had hesitated a moment before saying the name. In my overwrought state, I could have believed that he knew my real name and that I was not overproud of it, that day. As I returned to the other injured man, Adam was taking something from the box—I could not see what; and he began to mutter in a low voice. I felt an intruder and was glad to get back to the other bench.

The miner, who had led the way through the fall of stone and coal, said, 'Give us a hand with him. And let's hurry up: you never can tell when there's going to be another blower.'

Together we managed to carry him to the eye. There I did little more than watch my companion, who seemed to know exactly what he was doing, improvise a cradle for the wounded man out of two corves lashed together. We got Davie into it in a sort of sitting position and I held him while the other man tied his shoulders to a block of timber somehow fixed to the hook of the rope, and curled his legs into the corves. Then he signalled to the man on top: all the time we had been so alone in the pit there had been anxious watchers on top. Davie swung slowly upwards and, as my eyes tried to follow him, I realized that it must be dark for I could see nothing up there but a solitary red star.

When the rope came down again there was a man on it. Others were going to take over the task of bringing the rest of the injured to the surface: our work was finished. Adam had joined us and it was he who told the new-comer that there were no more injured: only dead men. They made me go to the surface next. A handful of men waiting to go down the shaft; a group round Davie; a few women waiting for news: these were all I could see in the smoking light of a torch. All idle spectators had gone. For a second everything seemed still: only the torch guttered in the night wind. They had waited so long: I had to tell them quickly.

'Only him,' I said, 'only Davie.'

Only one of the women moved, a girl who broke into a passion of weeping. Then they moved round her, to comfort her, while they waited—only a little while to wait now—for the bodies of their men.

Some of the men came to me, with ale and bread and bacon, and as I ate, asked about what we had found down there. I knew none of the men and none of them knew me but there was no strangeness between us. I told them all there was to be told and I asked about Davie.

'Come and see,' said one of them, and I went with him.

Davie had been laid on his belly and was lying with his mouth over a hole which had been newly dug in the earth. A man was astraddle him and pressing rhythmically somewhere just below his shoulder-blades.

'What's he doing? Won't that hurt him?' I asked. My companion looked surprised. 'Why, he's pressing the choke-damp out of him, back into the ground. That's where it came from in the first place, isn't it?'

This seemed reasonable and sure enough, the earth had soon sucked back the choke-damp out of Davie's body, and his breathing grew stronger and at last he began to suck in air like a thirsty man. They turned him over on to his back, then raised him into a sitting position. His eyes opened, roved over the watching faces, then stayed on one.

'What's up, mother?' he said.

'Never mind. Drink this first, son,' she said. She refused to let him say any more until he had emptied a large pot of ale, which he immediately vomited.

'Good lad,' she said with satisfaction. 'That's fettled the rest of it. And now you're coming home to your bed. But not before you've thanked this lad here,' and to my embarrassment, for I had not been aware that she realized I was there, she turned to me and said, 'What do they call you, lad?'

I almost blurted out my real name but stopped in time. 'Ralph. Ralph Reede.'

'Ralph Reede,' she repeated. 'I'll never forget it, not if I live to a hundred. And don't you forget the name of Agnes Fenwick. There'll be a place for you in my house as long as I live, if ever you want it, Ralph Reede. And don't you forget it,' she concluded, almost fiercely. I never claimed the place, but I know it always was there.

She said no more to me, but gave her attention to taking her son home, while the rest of the watchers moved towards the shaft, where the first body had just been brought to the surface. Suddenly I found I could bear no more. I turned to the man who had taken charge of me and asked if he could show me the way back to the cottage where I was staying. He was disappointed to have to leave but he agreed willingly enough, and we left the torchlight and stumbled through the workings and over the fields to the cottage.

The woman of the cottage was up, waiting for me with food and a cheerful fire, but she saw I was beyond talk and only asked me who had been rescued alive. I told her. She only sighed, and stared into the fire, and I remembered that she was the widow of a pitman. Then she turned to me and said, 'Would you like a bite to eat, Ralph?' I told her that I had had food and wanted nothing but my bed. So she gave me my rushlight and said she would go along the street and sit with her neighbour to wait for Adam's return.

I was so tired that I could scarcely hold up my head—or keep my eyes open, yet as soon as I was wrapped up in my blanket, I became wide awake. I kept my eyes shut, and they were hot and sandy under the lids, but my mind kept on going over and over what I had seen that day. The twisted sprawl of the first dead miner I had found; the smell of burnt flesh; Adam bending mysteriously over the dying man; Davie swinging helplessly up the shaft; the look on the women's faces, on the face of the woman whose cottage I was in: these and many other impressions of the day rose without order and began to tangle in my mind at last until Davie's mother looked at me with my own mother's eyes, and it was Thomas Trumbell's voice that called me a good lad, and when I finally fell asleep it was to find myself at a family meal in the Close, with my uncle, Sir Nicholas, fat in yellow satin, inveighing against the cost of mining coal, and waving a plump hand daintily clutching one of his favourite cinnamon comfits.

'It costs too much to win the coal from the pits,' he was saying. 'The price is too high. You'll soon find that out when you come into the business, Ralph, my boy. Won't he?'

And the others round the table nodded wisely in agreement, as they turned and stared at me.

Chapter 12

We were to have left Blyth early the next morning, yet when I awoke I knew that I had slept late: my head had the dull ache of too much sleep, and though there was little light at any time in the loft where I slept, it was full of the small sounds of a house awake. The cough in the room below was that of a woman awake; then a fire was being raked out; then came the sound of water being poured. I raised myself on my elbow: no sign of the widow's two sons who shared the loft. Why had no one woken me?

Then I remembered the accident. I got up, found my clothes and was soon in the room below. The woman of the house had heard that I was astir and had waiting for me the morning bowl of barley porridge and draught of cold well-water. Adam had left word, she said, that I was to have my sleep out, for we should not be going on to Bedlington that day, after all. 'You don't look really rested even now, Ralph,' she said, 'though you should: it must be fast on to midday.' And indeed the light coming through the open door was strong.

As I ate, I heard more about the pit accident. She had been one of the women who had laid out the bodies of the men. I gathered that this was one of the ways the widow managed to eke out a living. She promised me something from the dead men, to bring me good luck. She had been silent enough the night before: now, nothing could hold her tongue. Omitting nothing, she gave me an account of the injuries the bodies bore, and compared them with those of men dead in previous accidents, including her own husband. She paused for a moment. 'He made a lovely corpse,' she said, and she wiped away an easy tear with the corner of her apron. How could people have so little feeling? I wondered.

I asked myself this later in the day when I accompanied Adam to the arval for the dead miners. Judging by the noise issuing from the open door of the barn where the bodies were, it might have been a wedding feast we were going to, not an arval. It was a strange scene inside the barn: the foreground was thronged with men and women, youths and girls, children, even babies, all in their Sunday clothes; chattering, laughing, drinking and eating: all heedless of the still figures at the far end of the barn and the flickering candles in whose beams danced the dust of last year's harvest.

The shouts and laughter lulled as we entered, but had risen to a new crescendo before I had risen from the short prayer which I said in front of the waxen figures lying among the wild field flowers on the straightening board, each wrapped in its white shroud, with its face covered with a small square of white linen: on each breast was set the customary trencher with salt, and the lighted candle that guttered from time to time when the mourners grew boisterous. Adam removed the linen square and kissed each still face, but though I knew it was expected of me also, I turned away after a fleeting glance at the mutilated flesh and was glad of the tankard put into my hand by a woman whose face I half-remembered from the night before. I accepted also the white bread and baked meat offered me, for it would have been an affront to the dead to refuse, but though I had had little meat since I had left the house in the Close, both it and the fine white bread had little flavour for me, though the rest of the company were making the most of the unexpected feast.

At first the mourners made good-humoured attempts to draw me into their fellowship, but as I was not in a mood to respond they soon forgot me in the exchange of gossip and reminiscence that, as the ale went round again and again, became more and more laced with bawdy jokes. At last I could endure it no longer and slipped away full of disgust from the macabre merrymaking without a word even to Adam, who, talking quietly in a corner, seemed not to be aware that the scene was growing wilder each minute.

I spent the rest of the evening wandering through the few streets of the tiny town and in the little harbour at the river mouth staring at the fishing boats and the solitary collier getting ready to leave on the ebb tide. I was engulfed in a flood of homesickness and regret that I had, by my own folly, been cut off from my own people and forced to live among uncouth strangers. Because I have said little so far about my feelings during this time, you must not imagine that I had none. True, there had been moments when fear for my own life had driven out all other emotions: true, I had already begun to find it possible to be absorbed in the craft of healing that Adam practised; but most of the time I was two persons: Adam's assistant who went through the processes of a new way of living as if I had never known any other, and a second self, half-submerged but still longing painfully and passionately for the people and places I had lost. Even, at times, I seemed to have no identity at all. This was how I felt on that miserable evening, and if I had seen Harbottle Grimston himself walking straight towards me, I doubt if I should have cared enough to turn my face away.

It had grown quite dark: I could not stay out all night. I went back to the widow's cottage. There was no one at home: they were all still at the wake, but I could get in, of course: in all the places where I stayed, no one ever locked or bolted a door. On the stool near the hearth, where I would be sure to see it, there was a platter of meat and white bread which must have come from the arval of the dead miners. I knew it had been put there for me, but I went off to bed leaving it untouched. I did not want their kindness.

Next morning the widow called me as usual by thumping, from the room below, the floor beneath my pallet. I had by now come to my senses and realized that nothing could be more stupid than my anger with the only friends I had, and climbed down the ladder to the living-room, shamefaced and awkward. However, nothing was said about the previous day either by the widow or Adam, who had come in from his lodging near by. Adam and I had never yet been lodged in the same house. If I had not been so full of my own anxieties it might have occurred to me, before it in fact did, to wonder why.

I hoped that the fine food I had rejected yesterday would be set before me now, but I broke my fast with the barley broth which I was beginning to realize was the staple fare of ordinary people. The meal was a quiet one. I would have welcomed the widow's garrulity but for once she was disinclined to talk. Adam, too, was unusually quiet. I was glad to escape to bring Jennie to the door and load her panniers for our journey.

The widow revived somewhat at the moment of our departure and with something like her usual animation pressed gifts upon us. Adam accepted, as if it was a purse of gold from a departing monarch, a pair of clumsy shoes. My gift was a pair of thick stockings of undyed homespun, soles and heels discoloured but not too much darned. I was embarrassed by the unexpected gift and still Ralph Cole enough to be repelled by the thought of wearing stockings which had been worn by somebody else before, though badly furnished with clothes as I now was, they would be useful indeed. Instinctively I made to refuse the gift. Fortunately, the widow misunderstood my motive.

'No, go on lad: you take them, you can do with them. I can spare them. Anyway, they'll bring us both good luck,' she said.

So, ashamed, I took them, and tried to thank her properly.

When we had left Blyth and passed the churchyard with its row of raw, new graves, I plucked up courage to speak to Adam—we had been unusually silent that morning.

'What did she mean, that they'd bring good luck to both her and me?' I asked.

He stared at me for a moment before replying, 'They were on one of the miners before she laid him out for burial. I thought you'd have known that.' He must have seen the revulsion in my face. 'But then, there's a lot you don't know and don't like about simple folk, isn't there, Ralph?' His tone was kind, as if he pitied my lack of understanding. Then, to my utter amazement, without even knowing I was intending to do it, I suddenly found myself pouring out my story to him from the moment I had left the Close until last night when I had found the funeral merrymaking more than I could endure. He let me finish my story without interrupting. There was a little pause.

Then, 'I'm glad you've told me, Ralph,' he said. Another pause. 'I hoped you would.'

It was a few seconds before the impact of this filled my drained brain.

'You hoped.... You mean you've known all along?'

'Aye, Ralph. Kit told me that first day he met me in the Bigge Market. He didn't think it would be fair to saddle me unbeknownst with such a dangerous young outlaw;' the wrinkles round his blue eyes deepened. 'A poor lad not long out of the Marches, and not over-bright! Nay, Ralph, you're no player: I doubt you ever will be.'

I was mighty relieved that the play was over—at least as

far as Adam was concerned, yet so perverse is human nature that in less time than it takes me to put it into words, I was feeling foolish that I had been playing my part—and playing it not too well, it seemed—for an audience not taken in at all. Just as quickly again my feeling of foolishness was succeeded by vexation with those who, I thought, had made a fool of me.

'But why did you let me pretend? Why didn't you tell me you knew? Why didn't Kit? Or Archie?' I asked, and I do not think that I succeeded in keeping my vexation hidden.

'Well, if you must know, Ralph, we weren't too sure how you'd ... bring yourself down to the part you would have to play. "Thinks a sight too much of himself: too high and mighty by far," I think were Kit's words. Or were they Archie's?' He gave me a sly look to see how I was taking this estimate of my character. They were Kit's not Archie's, I was sure.

'... and we thought that if you had to pretend all the time, even to me, you might learn the part well enough to get by. After all, I would be the only one you would be with any length of time. I think Kit had some idea that it'd help to make you *feel* more like a poor travelling pedlar and get rid of some of the rich man's son's notions that might give you away.'

Rich man's notions? I began to feel my indignation rise again. Rich? For years I had lived with the idea that we were poor and forced to live in ways far beneath us.

Adam had an uncanny way of reading my thoughts.

'But it hasn't yet, has it, Ralph?' He sighed a little. 'Ah, well, I reckon you'll have to live poor a while longer before you have much fellow feeling with poor folk.' That was the only reference he made to my behaviour of the previous day and yet, for once, he was wrong: I *was* beginning to see the sufferings of the poor. 'Well, Ralph, we'll go on as before. We'll neither of us ask any questions: we'll just be what we seem to be. Let's leave it at that, eh?'

So it was agreed, and he rested his hand on my shoulder for a moment, while Jennie jogged on ahead and took no notice of either of us.

Chapter 13

There followed days of peace and sunshine. The weather, dull and sodden for so long, had changed and one golden day came after another so that all my memories of that time are bathed in warmth. And in calm; for Adam took peace and strength wherever he went. In those days God was for ever in men's mouths: Adam used the name sparingly and usually in one particular phrase. The first time I remember his using the phrase was that morning outside Blyth when I told him my story and my fear. 'We are all in God's hands,' he said. That was all Adam needed to know, and when I was with him that was all I needed to know. In no one else had I ever seen such faith. He did not speak of it: it emanated from him in calmness and strength. That was why he was such a good doctor: his patients drew strength from his calm hands and quiet eyes. Whether he had had much training in medicine or surgery, I never knew. I kept my bargain and never asked him questions about himself. But he performed cures which even now I, with all my learning and experience, remember and, remembering, am guilty of the sin of envy. I think he was the one truly good man I ever met.

Slowly we travelled north. Always Adam was looked for, always welcomed gladly. Sometimes the people had been afraid he might not come this year, because of the new war. 'Nay, you know better than that,' said Adam. Once he added, 'The year when I do not come you will know that I am dead or . . .' then checked himself with a shake of the head which I could have imagined was towards me.

Now that I had no secrets from Adam and I was growing fond of him, I settled into a peaceful routine, my fear of Harbottle Grimston, though never completely gone, subsided, and my sickness for home grew less unruly.

Then there began to be moments when I found myself noticing strange details and asking myself questions about Adam. He was not a Northerner: his speech showed that. How was it that for years he had spent part of each summer moving from village to village through the southern half of

Northumberland? And where did he spend the rest of the year? That he was an educated man soon became apparent to me. Where had he got his learning, and why was he content to do such a humble job? Then, he had lived abroad—in the Low Countries, for he could entertain me with accounts of customs there, and I had an impression that he knew something of Italy also. The man was full of mysteries. I discovered, moreover, that he was held in respect, not only by simple countrymen, fishermen, miners, and their wives, some of whom he had known as children, but that at some places, especially as we travelled farther from Newcastle, he visited the local gentry. At one village, the local squire had ridden in to meet him.

Moreover, I sensed that there was a special bond, something more than the usual one between doctor and patient, between him and some, not all, of the people we met. It was difficult to define this bond but that it existed I became increasingly sure.

Perhaps the most puzzling thing was that Adam and I were never lodged in the same cottage. At first I had accepted without question the explanation given each time that there was not enough room, but by the time that we had gone as far as Amble, I knew that on occasions there *had* been room for me in the same cottage as Adam. And why, I was now asking myself, did he always put me in the care of some young man while he himself disappeared? Was it the young man's job to see that I had no opportunity of finding out what Adam was doing? It would have been a poor return for Adam's kindness and protection to spy on him, but I began to be so consumed with curiosity that, if I had had the opportunity, I think I would have been prepared to do it.

I was learning to love the man. He knew all about me: could he not, in his turn, trust me? Then once more I would answer myself with another question: why was I so certain that he had a secret? And once more I would be hard put to it to express my suspicions in any really convincing form. So I went round in weary circles: and I could never shake off my doubts completely. And deep in my mind was forming a suspicion so full of danger that I never admitted it to my conscious thoughts at all.

Most of the golden days of that August had slipped away by the time we reached the hamlet of Amble. There we felt the ripples of the fresh wave of fear and despair that now washed over Northumberland. It was at Amble that we learnt that yet another army of Scots, undaunted by the news of the recent disaster of Preston,* had crossed the Border.

My first impulse was to turn and make for Newcastle as quickly as possible. I had lived all my life there, wrapped in the safety of its walls, protected by its narrow chares, warmed by its crowds. The countryside suddenly seemed cold and unfriendly. The peace I thought I had won during the short weeks with Adam proved suddenly shallow. But it did not appear to occur to Adam to do anything but go on his way as usual; and reason told me that Newcastle held no safe place for me now.

Then we ourselves came close to the Scots. Adam's route was taking us inland now. After leaving Amble we came to Felton, on the main highway between Edinburgh and Newcastle. Here we learnt that the Scots had been in the village only two hours before. They had spent the night there, taken all the grain and cattle they could find, and then left for Morpeth. So now there was an army between me and my home. There might be another siege of Newcastle at any time, and I would be shut out. There were times when it was hard to keep my mind on the work Adam gave me to do.

Day by day we journeyed westward now—and nearer the Marches. Every village we passed through seemed to lie under a crushing burden of fear: fear of the Scots, fear of the Royalists, fear of the Roundheads, fear of mosstroopers, and fear of winter: and all these were but different aspects of the greatest fear of all—fear of starvation. The pressure of their fears, added to my own that I could speak about only to Adam, at times well-nigh threatened to crush me.

Then my fear of capture became active again because at the village of Rothbury, high in Coquetdale, we came within the range of Roundheads, for the first time since our odyssey began. Parliament had not enough men to garrison all the captured castles of Northumberland but it did keep a small troop at Cartington Castle (where my cousin George Selby had

* The Battle of Preston was fought on 21 August 1648. The combined forces of Scottish Royalists under Hamilton and Northern Royalists under Langdale were defeated by Parliamentary forces under Cromwell. It was the major, and decisive, battle in the North of the Second Civil War.

been captured earlier that summer) because it was believed that fugitive Royalists had been seeking refuge with the moss-troopers of Tynedale and Redesdale. The Cartington Round-heads could not keep a watch on all ways to the Middle Marches but their unheralded descents on to different villages had, the Rothbury people told us, caught more than one Royalist, and kept the whole area in a state of tension. Cartington was not far from Rothbury, not as Roundheads used to travel.

If I had not known this, the pretty, remote village might have seemed a haven of peace, but as it was its very calm seemed malignant: its purple hills held a threat, and even the bleat of a distant sheep or the wail of a curlew might mean that Roundheads were abroad.

That evening as we ate our evening meal of nettle broth with the Shaftoes, a shepherd, his wife and two sons, at whose cottage Adam was to stay, Adam told us he had decided to cut short our time in Rothbury, where he usually spent two or three days, and leave early next morning for Elsdon, which he visited each year, though the law-abiding folk at Rothbury always thought that mosstroopers might well be left to look after themselves. I would gladly have left that very night, for Elsdon was the headquarters of the Middle Marches and even the Roundheads had always left the Borderers alone.

Shortly afterwards, Adam left the cottage with all the Shaftoes except the younger son, who stayed by the fire with me. He was busy making a crook. I had work to do also. Part of the late afternoon I had spent with a village lad on the flats down by the river, gathering thistle heads: Adam used the hard base of them in one of his simples. Now I was preparing the thistles, putting the down into a basket and the base on the hearth to dry.

The warmth, the quiet, the mechanical job I was doing, were combining to make me drowsy in spite of my nervousness. I was on the point of saying that I would go to my cottage to bed when the door was opened without the usual preliminary hail. Adam and the Shaftoes came in, out of breath.

'Come on, Ralph,' said Adam, 'we're going to Elsdon now. No, come just as you are; there's no time to waste. Keep with Rob here: he'll take you. We'll have to separate. You'll have a better chance that way: it's not you they're after. Hurry, lad.'

By the time I had snatched up my doublet the Shaftoes had opened the backdoor, which opened straight on to the hillside. But it was too late: already there was a clatter outside. Then Redcoats spilt across the little room. At the sight of them my heart stood still. Yet there was bewilderment in my terror. Why was the man at the front of the soldiers not a soldier at all, but a tall, thin spider of a man in black? He made straight for me: Adam's words of reassurance must have been mistaken. He grabbed me by the arm so tightly that it hurt.

Instinctively I tried to shake off his hand, but he was not Emmet nor yet a boy at school. The man, whoever he was, took my other arm as well, shook me until I was dizzy, then let go so suddenly that I stumbled and fell and my head hit the edge of the hearthstone. It was a minute before I could gather myself together enough to get on to my feet again. I was half dazed by the blow on my head and by bewilderment as well as fear. What was taking place was not quite what I had expected —in my imagination I had lived only too often through the moments when I should be recaptured. The one fear I had never dared to admit to my thoughts began to waken.

In a stupor, I heard the man's words. 'There you are,' he said. 'That's the one to go for: he's new to it.' To what? 'You'll get naught from them,' he stared at the Shaftoes; then he turned and spat at Adam and I felt myself flinch; 'nor yet from . . .' and even before he said them the dangerous words formed in my heart, '. . . a Papist priest.'

He was looking at Adam, hatred dark in his eyes. I too was staring at Adam, waiting, hoping to hear him deny the charge which could bring him—and those with him, I suddenly remembered—to a hideous death. Even as I waited, I knew with noon-day certainty that the charge was true. It was the one explanation that completely answered all my questions about Adam. I think that I must have known it all along underneath my own anxieties. I forgot all the kindness and patience of the man and the love I had come to feel for him: and like his dark enemy I too hated him. Because he had made a fool of me, taking my secret and keeping his own; because the feeling of security he had given me melted like the first snowflake on a cobblestone, and he was the most dangerous companion I could have had. He was my enemy and I was between him and my other enemies.

Then I thought no more of Adam: let him think of himself. My brain raced to find a way out of this new disaster but found none. If I gave up the pretence I had been living the last few weeks, I should have to become Ralph Cole again, Royalist fugitive, to be sold into slavery. Yet, anything was better to be than Ralph Reede, travelling companion of a travelling priest, one of that band who had kept the old religion alive in the Borders and the North ever since Queen Elizabeth's day.

These thoughts rushed, scarcely formed, almost it seemed through my blood not my mind, even as the fanatical Presbyterian—for such the man must be—was making his accusation. I wondered how he had found out what Adam was. Yet rather was it surprising that Adam's secret had not been discovered before. Perhaps it had: men might be more tolerant in the Borders where life was hard and they might need each other.

My thoughts raced so fast that the whole scene was slowed down—Adam, the Shaftoes, the soldiers, the Presbyterian, became unreal, people seen through glass, moving, talking, but unheard and unheeding. I think I only came to myself again when, with wrists tied behind my back, my body bruised by ungentle hands, I was hoisted on to a horse. A trooper mounted behind me and we rode at a steady pace through the darkness. I can remember the jingle of harness; the muffled pounding of the horses' hooves on soft ground; the smell of the sweat of horse and man; the night breeze on my face; the intolerable strain of riding with hands imprisoned; the fear of falling beneath the horses' hooves, a small fear that I let grow because it blessedly thrust out the other greater fears: then, at last, lights in the distance and a change in the sound and rhythm of our horses' feet: new voices; cressets; a courtyard. Then once again castle walls smelling of age and suffering and death loomed above me.

What was happening to the others I did not know but I was hustled along stone passages meagrely lit by an occasional cresset, brought to a halt, then, at last, led, blinking, into a bright room, warm and smoky from a peat fire smouldering in front of a reredos. A man was sitting at a table, talking to the black-suited Presbyterian. He was a large man, and his face was sickeningly familiar. I knew that I was lost, for he was the man I had hoped far away on the Tyne, the one Roundhead who really knew me—Harbottle Grimston.

He looked at me for a moment—I could tell that I was a part of the report the Presbyterian was making—and there was not a flicker of recognition in his gaze. I was thinner, browner, less well-clad than when he had known me in the house in the Close. It could be—yes, it could be—that he did not recognize me. It began to seem like a miracle.

At last they stopped talking. Harbottle Grimston, a captain now I noticed, promoted no doubt for zeal in hunting down Royalists, motioned the other to a seat beside him, and turned towards me. I braced myself for questions. At first sight of him, I had decided that there was nothing for me to do but to tell the truth, but when he did not recognize me, I decided to tell the story long ago agreed on with Kit and Archie. I might still be able to save myself. I hoped Adam would tell the same story: I thought he would because, when we had discussed the possibility of trouble with the Roundheads, we had agreed to stick to that story.

'Name?'

'Ralph Reede.'

It came without hesitation: I had been Ralph Reede for some time now.

'Of . . .?'

'Elsdon.'

And all the questions about myself I answered as I had answered in all the interrogations I had conducted in my own head since the story had first been decided on. The answers came easily. My interrogator gave no sign whether he believed me or not, but I had lived with my lie for weeks. It would be hard to get evidence to disprove it: Elsdon was not open to Roundheads; Tynemouth was a long way away, and Roundheads were too few and too valuable in Northumberland to send at this stage after evidence concerning a boy. I was more humble than I used to be and I could see that at this moment I was not very important to them for my own sake, only in so far as I might provide evidence against Adam. That was something I could not do, even if I wanted to—and there were moments that night when I might have been tempted to, if it would have bought my own safety. But Adam had been too cunning, I thought then (later I realized he had not been cunning, only kind and wise not to burden a fifteen-year-old boy with dangerous knowledge).

120

The questions soon turned to Adam. I felt easier now: I knew I could not provide a single piece of real evidence that Adam was other than he had seemed to be, a pedlar of herbs and medicines of his own making, with some skill in surgery. And even now, when I thought I hated him, I was glad of it.

Yes, I admitted, he *could* be what the Presbyterian claimed. But, I added, he could have been other things as well—a Royalist spy; a priest of the Church of England—*they* had been driven from their parishes, *they* held forbidden services in secret. Anything was safer to be than a Popish priest, I kept on reminding myself.

No, I had never seen a rosary or anything suspicious in his possession. Even as I denied it, there flashed into my mind a picture of the moments with the dying miner in the pit disaster at Blyth; I faltered for the flicker of a candle, then went on confidently. No, he carried no books, no papers, only medicines. No, he had not been out all that evening. Yes, he did sometimes go out at night. No. No. Yes. Yes. The questions went on and on, and always in the same calm, quiet almost tired voice. I had expected him to shout and bully. He was somehow different from the man I remembered. He did not refute any of my answers. My confidence grew. I was a match for this man after all. I felt the muscles in my neck and stomach gradually unknot themselves. Then, without any change of tone, and without any warning, came a question I had not been expecting:

'And where did you get the scars on your hands and on your cheek?' Involuntarily I glanced at my hands, at the marks left by some of the cuts and deeper grazes made by the rocks over the wall of Tynemouth Castle. 'Was it—maybe—at Tynemouth . . . Ralph Cole?'

So he had known all along, the devil.

In my anger and disappointment I took a step towards him. At the same moment as the guard seized me, a growling, snapping fury leapt at me from under the table. It was the queer unmistakable little mongrel I had last seen with Ambrose Grimston. So he *was* dead: the dog would never have left him otherwise. And the brother who had killed him must have found the dog in our quarters and recognized it and kept it. Harbottle Grimston had left his chair and picked up the angry little creature and was holding it in his arms. He stroked it

121

gently and it licked his hand lovingly. It was hard to believe he was the man I used to know.

He motioned to the guard. 'Take him away: he'll tell the truth tomorrow,' he said.

But there was no triumph in his voice: only infinite weariness, and a wish to be done with all of us.

Chapter 14

The footsteps of the guard seemed to walk a long way before they became too faint for me to hear. The silence that settled on me was as nearly tangible as the darkness in the cell. The smoky light of the Roundhead's torch had shown me nothing but a stone floor, a stone wall, and a heavy wooden door. I was too exhausted to do anything but slump to the floor. Too dispirited to think, I fell asleep.

How long I slept there was no way of knowing, for it was as dark and silent as before when I slowly came to myself again. I was cold: cold and with an ache in all my bones. The sleep, however, must have done me good. I got to my feet and, I scarcely knew why, fumbled my way along the wall. It was not long, only a few paces, before I came to a corner, and then another, and another, and then my fingers felt wood, and a metal lock, colder, if that were possible, than the stone walls. I had come to the door of the cell. I completed the circuit of the walls, which was very small, then tried walking across the cell. There was not a pallet, not even a stool to sit on. I wondered if there were any kind of window opening. It seemed unlikely: surely even on the darkest night even the smallest slit would show less dark than the rest of the walls. Nevertheless, I felt my way round the cell once more, this time with hands high above my head, feeling for any opening there might be. There was only one, the small grill in the massive door. I pressed myself as close to it as possible, eyes and ears straining. Nothing: not a glimmer of light, not an echo of a voice. Then in a sudden panic, I pounded at the door with my fists and screamed senselessly through the grill. No one came. The silence that drifted down again like soot was broken only by my own rough breathing and the pounding of blood in my ears.

I was completely alone with my thoughts. My fear had subsided now. I realized that it was after all to my advantage that Harbottle Grimston had recognized me. He would know that I was a Royalist, but not a Papist. The plantations or the galleys would be my lot; at that moment either seemed infinitely preferable to the punishment that might have been mine—and would certainly be Adam's. He would be taken to Newcastle and put to the torture to make him reveal the names of other Papists, other priests: Adam would never tell. He was an old man; perhaps he would die on the rack. Best for him if he did, for if he survived, he would at the last be dragged on a hurdle through unfriendly streets to the gallows, and in front of a gaping holiday crowd, he would be hanged, then taken down alive and disembowelled. His poor, humiliated body would be displayed in different parts of the city and his kind old head nailed to the bridge, until it ceased to bear any resemblance to the gentle healer I had known, or to anything human at all.

Then, like a blow from a fist, without warning the thought came to me that Adam might have got away safely if he had not come back to the cottage for me. And I had hated him. Not for long, but I had hated him. I could not bear to be still and I got to my feet and walked up and down the tiny cell.

There was no way of measuring the time that had passed when I noticed that the darkness seemed less complete; that I could see the grill in the door showing as a barred square less black than the rest of the cell. There were no other signs of day: no stir of movement, no sounds of men or animals, though not for a second did I cease to listen.

At last I heard footsteps. The steps grew louder, then stopped. There was a light outside the grill in the door. A key fumbled into the lock: there was a grating noise and the heavy door was pushed slowly open. I took a deep breath, holding the air pressed firmly against my ribs for a second or two to keep myself from trembling. Not long now, and my own fate would be settled. I had no thought of escape. All I hoped was that I should not incriminate my mother, or Kit, or Archie. Adam I could not incriminate: I knew nothing incriminating about him, though I had no doubt that the charge was true.

The Roundhead soldier tied my wrists behind my back and motioned me to walk in front of him, and we went along the cold passage-way, then up stone stairs so narrow and twisting that, with my hands behind my back, I had to tread very slowly for fear of falling. My guard gave me an impatient prod between my shoulder-blades and told me to 'get a move on: they hadn't all day'. This was the only thing he said to me from the moment we met until the moment we parted.

'If you want me to hurry on these stairs, you'll have to untie my hands,' I said. There was no need to be civil to a Roundhead any more. I had the sour pleasure of knowing that nothing I said or did now could make my lot any worse.

I had supposed that I was being taken for my trial, or possibly for further questioning, perhaps to the room I had been in the night before, although I had no memory of coming down these narrow stairs. To my surprise, however, we presently emerged into a big courtyard, bright with sunlight and full of movement. At first I had to screw my eyes up against the light, but soon I could see that in the courtyard a troop of Roundheads was mounted and ready to ride. Each man was carrying his full equipment. This could not be an ordinary patrol. What was happening? And why had I been brought out here?

I looked around. Almost the whole garrison must be here:

we knew from talk in Rothbury that it was only a small one. There were two horses saddled but without riders. Then through a small gateway at the far end of the courtyard came a little group of figures: the officer I had seen last night, Adam, and, there was still no mistaking him, Harbottle Grimston. What I had begun to guess—that Cartington Castle was being abandoned by the Roundheads—must be true. If it were only a change of garrison taking place, prisoners would hardly be taken along. Anyway, there was not a sign of incoming troops.

But why? Why should Cartington be abandoned? What could have happened? Something important—and unexpected. Well, I should know before long: in a day or two at most: in an hour or two, maybe, if I kept my ears open.

Adam and I had been brought out at the last moment, obviously (where were the Shaftoes? I wondered). The troop was ready to ride. Adam and I were to be kept apart, I soon realized. He was hoisted on to the horse of Harbottle Grimston himself, at the front of the cavalcade, and I was mounted with a sergeant at the rear, but he managed to give me a reassuring nod, which shame for the feeling I had had for him when I had seen him last made me slow to answer. The order to start was given and we clattered through the main gatehouse only a minute or two after I had been led into the yard.

We set out at a brisk pace and in perfect order in what I judged to be an easterly direction, though living in Newcastle as I had done all my life, I could be put to shame by a five-year-old country lad in judging either direction or time from the sun. We must be making for Alnwick, or Berwick, then. I asked the sergeant who was mounted behind me where we were going, but his only reply was, 'On the Lord's errands,' which did not tell me very much.

The country we were riding through was the wildest I had yet seen: great stretches of open moorland, golden with dying bracken, purple with heather, and patched with the moving shadows of the bright clouds that drifted across the blue autumn sky. It was wide, open country, safe to ride over, for, apart from a solitary clump of trees away to the south, there was nothing bigger than a few straggling gorse bushes, not high enough to hide an ambush. A more empty stretch of country it would be hard to imagine.

Suddenly, from nowhere, stones rained down on us. The

126

front riders faltered and checked their horses: the neat column crumpled and became torn at the edges, and a terrified horse broke away at a gallop, his rider desperately trying to hold him in check. Then men, wild, screaming men, ragged and unkempt, sprang like devils from the earth itself, or materialized from the air, and were in our very midst among the plunging hooves. A red-haired creature with savage eyes and shouting a strange, barbaric cry, appeared at my side and dragged me from my horse. I saw the upward flash of a knife, and, amidst all that noise and confusion, I heard the deep groan of the soldier behind me. I fell to the ground, dragging him with me, and felt a warm gush on my neck, down my back. I glimpsed the wild stranger with arm raised to strike again. Then I felt a shattering blow on my head: and nothing more.

Chapter 15

The ceiling worried me. There was not much light for me to see by, only a little daylight turning pink, but surely the roof was vaulted, like a church's. I lazily followed the pattern of the ribs, but my eyes were hot and rusty-lidded. I closed them again: it was too much effort to stay awake.

Next time I opened my eyes the light was different; I could not see the ceiling at all: it was completely in shadow. I must raise my head. This time it was the bones of my head that were rusty, and they seemed to grate against each other as I moved, but I managed to lift myself enough to see that I was lying on a pallet on the floor of a fair-sized building—a church perhaps; the rushlights showed the bases of pillars. There were other figures lying on the floor near me and a woman was sitting not far away. The pain in my head was too great, and even that dim light hurt my eyes: I was glad to drop back on my bed.

Memory began to filter back again through my jagged skull: the ride out of Cartington; the ambush; the red-haired savage who had dragged me from the saddle. None of this told me where I was now, but I did not care very much and I drifted back into sleep.

Then, somehow, it was day, and as light as it ever is in an old church. I found I could sit up this time with scarcely a twinge of pain. I was even hungry. The woman I had seen during the night was still there: she was busy spooning porridge for a man not far from me whose right arm was heavily bandaged. She glanced up as I was reaching for my clothes, which I had noticed at the foot of my bed. I half-expected her sharply to order me to lie down again, but she was not Alyse, and she just gave me a nod of approval and went on with her job.

I was not as well as I had thought, and pulling on my clothes was exhausting work: when at last I had managed it, I was glad to sit on my bed and look around me. My pallet was the last of a row placed against the stone wall of what I guessed to be the left side of one of the church's transepts. There was another row facing it.

'All right. All right. Don't sit there gawping. Tidy your bed up, then go and get yourself some porridge.'

The woman believed in bullying her patients back to health; or else she was one of those nurses (I have met many of them since) who really only like people who are at death's door, to be snatched back by their hands. Feeling resentful, and hoping that she could see it, I smoothed the thin and dingy covers on my pallet; then, dizzy from bending, I straightened my back and waited for my eyes and ears to behave normally again before I began to pick my way between the two rows of pallets in the narrow transept to the centre of the church, where there was a trestle table, and another woman in charge of a cauldron of porridge. She was short and thin (I never saw a fat woman or man, that year, outside Newcastle) and full of energy. She knew my name, my real name, and rolled it with the richest burr I'd ever heard. I thought myself familiar enough with Northumbrian speech and would have said that it was not very different from Newcastle's, but the Border lilt, the Border version of Harry Hotspur's burr,* the Border idiom, was sometimes beyond me.

She was busy at that moment and stopped only long enough to give me my bowl of barley porridge and pull out a cracket from under the trestle, but she talked quickly and gave me no chance to feel shy.

'So you're awake at last, Ralph Cole,' she said. 'Not before time, neither, for there's nowt much wrong with you. You can thank Heaven for that thick brain-pan of yours.' She smiled at me. 'Sir Adam said,' she went on, and the old priestly title came naturally from her lips, 'Sir Adam said that that daft gowk, Red Armstrong, overdid it a bit when he fetched you that great crack on the head, that's all. Sup up your broth, me cannie lad, and just have a bit sit there till Sir Adam comes, and then we'll see what's next.' She ladled out another bowl of porridge and trotted off with it down the transept.

I was pleased enough to sit quietly and eat my porridge, the thinnest I had had yet. I was hungry. It was ... I realized I did not know how long it was since I had last eaten or how

---

* There is a legend that the Northumbrian burr, so-called, arose from the imitation by his followers of a speech peculiarity of Harry Hotspur.

long I had been at Elsdon, or how I had got here. The red-headed man who had pulled me from my horse might be responsible for my sore head, but it looked as if he was also responsible for rescuing me from the Cartington Roundheads. There were still gaps in the story of our rescue that I was piecing together, but in my lazy mood I was content to wait to fill them in later. However, this is as good a moment as any to give you the story.

As soon as Adam and I and the Shaftoes were taken away from Rothbury by the Roundheads, one of Adam's parishioners —yes, he *was* a priest of Rome—had slipped away from Rothbury and made for Elsdon. He knew Elsdon was to have been out next stopping-place. The man knew, of course, that there was a goodly number of fighting men gathered there. He had reached Elsdon during the night and given his news to the night patrol. The leader of the patrol had thought the news serious enough for him to leave his men and to waken the chief of the Redesdale men. At a council of war it was decided that an attempt must be made to release Adam—and the rest of us, though, as the story was told, it was clear that we were only of minor importance. As the chances were that Adam would be taken to Newcastle for trial, perhaps immediately, the attempt must be made at once. Accordingly, a band was mustered of able-bodied men, Borderers, who knew every inch of the moors between Elsdon and Cartington.

Before they reached Cartington, however, they received information that the garrison had received orders to leave. I must add here that during my stay at Elsdon I was constantly surprised to find how well-informed the men of the Marches were of events throughout Northumberland. A perpetual feud existed between them and their more peaceful neighbours in the lower valleys, but they seemed to have their spies there, and of course they themselves could come and go as swiftly and silently as mountain deer, and could vanish into the heather and rock as miraculously as a moorland snake. So, on this occasion, they knew that the garrison commander had received orders late that night to evacuate Cartington immediately and take his troopers towards Berwick to meet at some point General Cromwell who had, at last, reached Newcastle and was leaving it for Berwick.

This news had brought the rescue party to a halt and a quick change of plan was made. It was decided to make a surprise attack on the Roundheads in open country where they would not be expecting it. A small party was detached from the main body, all Redesdale men, the strongest and most fleet of foot, and able to find cover where no one else could. They were to conceal themselves on the open moor on the track near Cartington which the Roundheads would take if they were going to Berwick. They were to wait until the Roundheads were upon them before hurling their stones at men and horses; then snatch the prisoners and, counting on the confusion to give them a good start, make for the clump of trees south of the place of ambush. Here the rest of the party would be waiting on horseback to ride out and pick them up, and fight off the Roundheads, if any recovered from the surprise attack quickly enough to be dangerous. Red Armstrong, his brother, and two others had been part of the ambush party and they were to grab Adam and me and the Shaftoes and get out of the mêlée immediately—to knock us unconscious, if necessary, and carry us. Adam had been on the look-out for a rescue attempt—he knew his people—and the Shaftoes were not with us. Harbottle Grimston had turned them loose that morning: they were not worth cluttering up the column with. So three of the rescuers had easy work.

Red Armstrong had more to do. He told me (it was from Red that I got most of the story) that when I first clapped eyes on him, I looked as if Old Nick himself had jumped up from the mouth of hell, and he thought I might start an argument.

'That was no time for that,' he said apologetically, 'so I clouted you one, Ralph, and fetched you to Elsdon. Never did know me own strength,' he added, a trifle complacently it seemed to me.

However, I must get back to my main story.

I was glad to know that Adam was safe there in Elsdon, yet I felt shy of meeting him again. I might tell myself that he was the same Adam that I had travelled with the last weeks, that the revelation that he was a Papist priest had not changed him, but it had made me shy of meeting him again. What should I say? How should I begin? What should I call him?

I had not long to wait before seeing him again, and my anxiety had been quite unnecessary, because when Adam came he brought someone with him, a small figure unrecognizable for a moment, but only a moment, against the light of the open door.

'Jackie!'

I leapt to my feet, knocking over the stool and scarcely noticing the jagged pain in my skull.

'Aye, lad, it's good to see you.'

Jackie's pleasure, I do believe, was as great as mine: for a moment neither of us found anything else to say. We contented ourselves with a clasp of the hands, and Jackie gave me a friendly punch or two on the shoulders, while I was afraid I might cry like a baby. The sharp-tongued nurse, coming to the table with her empty porridge bowl, saved me, however, by informing us that if we were going to make any more noise she'd thank us to take ourselves outside and let the wind waggle our tongues where they couldn't disturb sick folk. 'Not you, of course, Sir Adam, begging your pardon, sir,' and she dropped him a curtsy.

Adam smiled and said that sounded a good idea. Jackie could show me Elsdon, and take me to pay my respects to my family. My family?

'The Reedes, Ralph, the Reedes. But don't keep him out too long, Jackie. He's not properly over that knock on the head your enthusiastic kinsmen gave him. I'll just have a look at you first, Ralph,' he said, and made me sit down again while he gently felt my head. 'You'll do,' he remarked, and dismissed me, but not before he had given me a gentle pat on the shoulder and a smile perhaps more kind even than usual. That was all the reference he made to what had happened since we had last talked together.

Looking back, I believe that he did not attach any special importance to the Rothbury-Cartington incident. He had lived in constant danger for many years and who knows what other escapes he had had. His faith made danger and death unimportant to him. He was a great man and you had never heard of him. The people who knew him grow fewer each year: soon there will be no one left to remember.

You can well imagine that Jackie and I had plenty to talk about, but what we said has nothing to do with this story.

That first morning, after visiting Mistress Reede, when Jackie and I walked through the village, it was to me a strange picture

132

from another world. In my wanderings through Northumberland I had never seen any village quite like Elsdon nor quite as poor. It was built round a large green—much larger than the number of houses seemed to warrant, but Jackie told me that Elsdon had long been the gathering place of the clans of the Middle Marches. The church was at the north of the village, and near it was a fortress-like stone building which Jackie said was the vicar's pele. When I asked what he meant he told me it was the home of the vicar, when the village had one.

'Looks more like a little castle,' I said stupidly.

'That's just what it is,' said Jackie. 'This is the Borders, Ralph, not comfortable Newcastle. Oh, aye; it's suited you all fine, since James came in, to call us all rievers and cattle thieves, and say it's time law was brought to the Borders, but we've always had our own law here, though it might not be the same as yours. Aye, it suits you all fine now to forget that for many a long year you left it to us rievers and cattle thieves to keep the auld enemy'—he glared savagely at a couple of bony-kneed Scots, sitting outside a hut, sharpening their dirks, and they stared back at him with as little love in their eyes—'off the backs of the fat aldermen in Newcastle. And all for the price of a few cattle, which nobody wanted to pay, and which at any time these three hundred years and more you'd hang us high for—if you could catch us.'

I had never suspected such thoughts in Jackie. He saw my gape of surprise.

'Take a good look round you, Ralph. Not much better than your swine-cotes, are they? And the chief's house,' he pointed to the one larger building, 'scarcely better than a Newcastle keelman's is it? Let alone an alderman's.'

Truth to tell, it scarcely looked as good as a keelman's: it was larger, but far more crudely built. Jackie seemed now to be talking to himself:

'But I'm not going back: not even if I have to starve to death, which is like enough this winter. Here I am my own man again.'

He looked beyond the village to the bare hills. For a moment I saw them with his eyes, and they were beautiful and free. Then he gave a little self-conscious laugh, and became the old Jackie again.

'Well that's enough of that. Come on, Ralph; we'll go and

meet my folks. You're going to stay with us as long as you're in Elsdon.'

We had to cross the green to get to his home. In ordinary times, the green would be an open space, but all the time I was in Elsdon it was as crowded as Bigge Market on a fair day. Everywhere there were old tents or rough temporary huts of wattle and mud. Space had been left round the cockpit (I saw two, maybe three, cock-fights while I was in Elsdon) but the rest of the green was filled.

As for the men outside the tents and huts, well, I doubt whether any other single place in the country could have produced such a varied collection. There were Scots, Highlanders by the look of their blue waistcoats and bonnets and their plaid cloaks, and I could hardly believe my eyes when I saw that they had bows and arrows. There were Borderers in simple homespun, and gentlemen Cavaliers, easy to distinguish by their tarnished lace and air of bedraggled splendour. There was a group of soldiers in the grey breeches and red coats of Parliament's army, sober-looking men, some of them busy cleaning and polishing muskets. These interested me most: Parliament men who turned coat could expect only death if they were captured. Some of them were carefully chipping stones.

'What are they doing that for?' I asked Jackie.

'Making them the right fit for their muskets, of course.'

Bows and arrows instead of muskets, stones instead of bullets: I think it was then that I finally gave up any lingering hope I might have had of a victory for the King.

'Come on, Ralph,' said Jackie. 'That's our Nessie, our Cud's wife, over there at her door. She's a fair blazor. But you'll not can help liking her, Ralph: she's a grand lass, as long as you're not a Scot.'

The grand lass was a middle-aged woman: tall, raw-boned, sandy-haired, wearing an almost white flannel petticoat and bodice, and on her head a kerchief, the corner unpinned and hanging loose. This homespun dress, I discovered, was almost a uniform among the women of Elsdon, worn even by the laird's lady, though she had a blue cloak to put over it when it was cold, whereas the village women had homespun shawls.

Nessie welcomed me very kindly. We went inside her cottage, down two or three stone steps, for the level of the floor was below the level of the ground outside, so that it was possible to stand upright in most of the building. The place was gloomy and so smoky that my eyes soon began to water. On this occasion I did not care to look too much around me, but I got to know the cottage very well eventually. It was the most primitive building I have ever lived in and all the cottages in Elsdon seemed to be built in the same way. Two upright tree-trunks, the bark still on them in places, with a horizontal one laid across them in forks at the top, formed the main structure of the hut. At the sides, thick branches of trees leant on the horizontal ridge, and at the ends these branches, which formed the rafters of the hut, rested on the upright posts, so that the rafters, all round, extended from the roof ridge right down to the ground. Low walls had been made inside, of wattle. There was a fair-sized hearth built into the thickness of the wall with a chimney above it made of rough-hewn stones, clawed out of the village quarry on the hill-side. Two muttons dangled in the smoke from the fire, getting more and more brown and dusty each day. Jackie told me, half apologetically, for we ate no meat while I was there, that they were for the Christmas feasting.

In the daytime everybody spent as much time as possible out of doors, for like all the houses in Elsdon the hut was even more crowded than usual, with Nessie and Cud and their two children, Jackie, and two Royalist soldiers. Now I was come to add to the crowding. I was accepted gladly. I was a friend of Sir Adam, of Jackie, of Archie, and therefore to be made one of Nessie's family and cuffed and cosseted accordingly. That first morning she gave me a mug of queer-tasting milk.

'A special treat, mind you, because you're still a mite pasty after the clout on the head that great gowk, Red, gave you. It'll be no good coming for any another day, because you'll get none. The sheep're running dry, and I want all their milk for cheese for the winter,' she said.

The winter. How often that word was on the lips of the country folk of Northumberland that year, 1648. I wonder how many survived that winter.

I suddenly found that I was tired and was glad to sit on the hearth and listen to Nessie and Jackie. In spite of the smoki-ness, I was comfortable with the fire warming my back and ordinary people who knew who I was talking in front of me.

135

As I drowsed, it almost seemed that I was in the great kitchen in the house in the Close, and that was Alyse's voice relishing the gossip, and I half-expected Emmet to come in and sit beside us with her needlework. Suddenly, a great wave of longing for home swept over me and I wished with all my heart that I had never run away.

Since Tynemouth I had been trying to live one day at a time, not letting my thoughts go either back or forwards, but now cruel regrets for my folly and fear of the future tormented me. In that friendly cottage with Jackie and his sister quietly talking, I felt alone and helpless. Jackie was back with his own people: mine seemed very far away. I felt like rushing out of the hut there and then, and setting off at once for home. It was bitter to know that once out of sight of Elsdon I would be lost and might wander in that wild country until I died of cold and hunger. I must depend on Adam or Jackie to make plans for me. What claim had I on them? Why should any man risk leaving the shelter of Elsdon for my sake?

Then I remembered the gold coins my mother had sent me. Elsdon was a poor place. There must be someone in it who, for a piece of gold, would take me at least as far as some road that would lead me to Newcastle; or to the Picts' Wall, which I could follow to the city. Then, surely, I could somehow get into the city and home again. That 'somehow' was not very convincing, but even so the thought of my gold pieces restored some of my confidence. These half-starved Borderers would do anything for a single one of them, I felt sure. I must go about the business carefully, that was all. I had to be sure that my money got me what I wanted and not a place in a bog with my throat cut. However, now I had even half a plan, I felt some of my homesickness disappear, and by the time I had finished the milk I was looking about me and listening to Nessie's gossip with the detachment of the visitor to a strange place who makes up his mind to like it because he knows he will soon be leaving. A few gold pieces could still make me feel vastly superior to Jackie and all the others I had met who had nothing to set against them except kindness and generosity and willingness to share the little they had.

Later in the morning I went back to the church where I found Adam still busy. He was an amazing man: he must have started work immediately he arrived in Elsdon. When I said this, he looked surprised.

'Well, of course,' he said; 'there's more sick and wounded folk here than usual this year.' His eyes glanced along the rows of pallets on the floor of the church. Then he turned to the table and pointed to the heaps of self-heal and comfrey. 'Do you feel up to work today, Ralph? Good. You'd best start on these then. There'll be plenty more wounds to be mended, I'm afraid. Then the fleabane: I never heard of an army yet that didn't get the flux. It hasn't reached here yet, but it will.'

He left me and went round the patients again, for he was shortly going back to the vicar's pele for the rest he took at midday in Elsdon whenever possible, so that he could attend during the night to the seriously ill who needed him. I was pleased that he had not asked if I knew how to prepare the herbs, and glad to have work to do instead of worrying about how I was to get away from Elsdon which, just a short time before, I had been afraid I might never reach.

Chapter 16

It was Adam who raised the subject of my return to Newcastle. Just before he sent me back to Nessie's cottage that evening, he said, 'You'll be wondering what you're going to do next.'

I said that I was.

'It's not going to be easy, Ralph, not at all easy. It's hard to know what's going to happen in these parts. The news seems to be that the latest lot of Scots have gone back over the Border—they didn't get farther than Morpeth; nobody seems to know why. Cromwell was in Felton two days ago and was going on to Alnwick. It looks as if he's going to follow the Scots or, maybe, once he's sure they're over the Border, all he'll do will be to try and take Berwick and leave the Scots to fight among themselves, which they've every sign of doing. Who can tell? In any case, Northumberland's not going to be a good place for travelling in yet awhile. What d'you think, Ralph? D'you think you should still try to get to Newcastle for St. Luke's Fair? Or would you like to stay here till spring? Either way, it's going to be a bit risky, I'm thinking. If Parliament does win back all the fortresses in the county, it might turn on this place: they've talked of it often enough. What do you say, Ralph?'

'I'd like to try to get home,' I said.

'That's what Jackie and I thought you'd say. Well, you're probably right. This place is for those born to it. Not that you wouldn't be welcome, Ralph,' he added, kind as ever, 'and not that you wouldn't earn what you ate but ... oh, well ...'

Adam had a knack of making me ashamed of myself. I remembered how, a few hours previously, my gold had seemed to make me superior to Jackie and Nessie and all Borderers. Was Adam able to read my thoughts, or did he just understand human nature very well? Or did my conscience sometimes read meanings into his words that he never intended?

'What are you going to do, Adam?' I said. (I never could bring myself to give him his priestly title, and I do not think he expected me to.)

'Stay here till all these troubles are over.' He sighed. 'I am just a danger wherever I go, now. I suppose the wonder is that it took so long for them to find me out. I wonder who that man was—I didn't know his face—and how he came to be at Rothbury. I suppose they have their spies, also.'

'Well, what about Jackie?' I said, anxious to make amends for my mean thoughts that morning. 'I'm sure my mother would find a place on a ship for him as well.'

'I'm sure she would,' said Adam, 'but don't you think you've given her enough to do looking after you? Anyway, Jackie's quite determined to stay here.'

'But what about Madge?'

'That's where you *can* help, Ralph,' he said. 'Jackie'd never ask for anything for himself, but if your mother could help Madge, take her back into service, maybe, or find her a place with one of her friends, that would repay anything the Armstrongs have done for you. Then maybe when peace comes again, Madge'll come and join Jackie in Elsdon.'

I promised that when, if, I did get back to the house in the Close, I would ask my mother to look after Madge.

'But how am I going to get back?' I added gloomily.

'Leave it to us: it'll be arranged somehow,' said Adam.

This was the moment to mention my gold pieces.

'Adam,' I said, rather hesitantly, 'I have three gold pieces. D'you think . . . ?'

It was growing dark in the church. I could not read the expression on his face.

'Only a man of the Marches can get you safely over the moors and on your way to Newcastle—only a riever knows the ways —and he'll not do it for three gold pieces or twenty, though he'll do it to oblige a kinsman. And there's only the Marchmen you can really be sure of in Elsdon. Any one of the others could be a spy for Parliament. So don't try anything on your own, Ralph. You'll just have to go on trusting us to do our best.'

With that I was content; at first, at least. Adam gave me plenty to do in the hospital. Moreover, Elsdon itself was perpetually buzzing with life, or at least with talk. Most of the refugees seemed to have little to occupy them except talk and quarrel. The Borderers themselves had plenty to do. They took their turns at standing watch over the ways into Elsdon and patrolling the moors. No one else was allowed to share these tasks. The men of the Marches knew the secret ways in and out of the dales and had no wish to share their secrets. It was the Elsdon men, too, who made the raids on the flocks and crops on the Scottish farms over the Border. From these raids the men returned angered by the meagreness of their booty and casting more and more resentful looks on the refugees who were fast becoming simply useless mouths to be fed rather than allies.

Not long after the report of Cromwell's presence in Northumberland had circulated, another handful of refugees rode into Elsdon. They were all that had escaped from Bamburgh, which had just been captured by a detachment of Cromwell's troops. They were received with little enthusiasm.

Then news trickled through (as news always did) that Berwick was besieged: then that terms had been reached and Berwick was to be surrendered to Cromwell. Then, worse still, it was reported that those terms had included an agreement that the Royalists should also deliver up Carlisle, apparently without a fight. This meant the virtual end of Royalist resistance in the North. Reports became more dismal still. The opposing parties in Scotland appeared to have settled their differences and Cromwell and Hazelrigg were said to be in Edinburgh making terms for the disbanding of all Scottish armies. The Second War was over.

According to Jackie there were many discussions between the head men of the Borderers and the Cavalier officers. The crowd on Elsdon green was thinning out. Some of the men I had passed often enough to say 'What cheer?' to were no longer there. Obviously some Royalists had decided to hang about no longer waiting for orders from Sir Marmaduke Langdale or any other of the King's generals.

As for me, I waited in an agony of impatience for Adam or Jackie to mention again the question of my own departure. By now we were into October and St. Luke's Fair began on the eighteenth of that month. I had made a pact with myself—I scarcely know why—that I would wait for them to mention the subject first. They, no doubt, assumed that I was trusting them and did not guess at my doubts. Each day that went by made it harder for me to keep my bargain with myself. Adam *must* have forgotten all about my escape.

Then, one afternoon, not long after midday, when the

patients were drowsing after the morning's ministrations, and when Adam usually left me and one of the village women in charge, instead of asking, as usual, if we could manage without him, Adam asked me to accompany him back to the vicar's pele.

As soon as we were outside the church he said, 'Well, to-night's the night, Ralph. It's all arranged.' He looked at me and smiled. 'Did you think it was never going to be? The man we've been waiting for has come at last and you'll be on your way before sunset. A couple of days ago we sent a message through that you'd be setting off about now. If it's got through, they'll know in Newcastle that you'll be coming by Hexham. Hexham's the best we can do for you, Ralph. From there, it's up to them.'

I was both relieved and excited by the news, and found time to wonder what would happen if the message had not reached Kit or my mother. Adam, in his old, uncanny way, answered the question I had not asked.

'If word didn't get through'—no hint how the message had been sent: I knew better, now, than to ask questions—'it'll be up to you, Ralph. You're better able to fend for yourself these days. Some day you'll even be able to fend for other folk,' he said, and his smile robbed the words of any sting they might have had.

Now that the moment I had been waiting for had come, I was strangely loth to go.

'Well, they're waiting for you at Nessie's,' he said. 'Good-bye, Ralph.' He stretched out his hand to me. I fell to my knees and kissed it, as I had seen his own people do. For a moment I was one of them, and hoped for his blessing, though I had no words to ask for it. 'God bless you, Ralph. Remember, you are in His hands.' He gently withdrew his hand and had gone before I could find my voice to thank him for so many things. I never saw him again.

Chapter 17

As I pushed open the door of Nessie's cottage, a delicious smell greeted me, or rather an assortment of smells: toasting cheese, onions, and—I must be dreaming—frying meat. Then I noticed the stranger sitting in the place of honour by the fire-place. He was not the sort that a man on a galloping horse would stop to look at, to use one of Nessie's expressions. Even if you saw him in a quiet street I doubt whether you would spare him a second glance, so completely ordinary was he: neither tall nor short; neither fat nor thin; neither fair nor dark. He was dressed in an equally neutral way: in a city he would have passed as one of the humbler citizens; in a village or on a country road as a modestly prosperous countryman. No one told me his name and he just nodded agreeably when Nessie said, 'Here's the lad: this is Ralph,' and went on talking to Jackie and Cud.

All the family were present, and Archie Reede's mother too. The children, out of respect for the stranger and for their mother's warnings not to get under her feet and make her spoil the haggitty, were trying to keep still on the stools where they had been planted. Usually, when I came home, Nessie was full of talk, but tonight she was preoccupied with her cooking and determined to do justice to such precious ingredients.

I had assumed that the unexpected feast was in honour of the stranger, but I was placed next to him and received a portion of the haggitty as big as his and distinctly larger than anybody else's; I was no longer one of the family: I was a guest again. Have you ever tasted a Northumbrian haggitty? Of course not: not a Border one, with the strange bite of smoked mutton to bring it to perfection. I will admit that it can be quite tasty with smoked bacon instead, but never quite as good as the one I ate in Elsdon. Perhaps you have to live on porridge and herbs for weeks on end really to appreciate that blend of cheese and onions and meat.

No one talked during the meal. Even the hot oatcakes which Nessie gave us straight from the girdle after the haggitty were too precious to be mixed with words. The children were slow to finish.

'They're each scared to finish first and have to watch the other with some left,' said Nessie, tolerantly. 'Come on, now, you two. If you won't finish it, there's others that will.'

The girl and boy gave her a reproachful look but emptied their bowls.

'All right,' said Nessie, 'you can't lick the bowls any cleaner. Run out to play now, but say good-bye to Ralph. He'll be leaving before sunset.'

They were Border children and of recent years had learnt to accept comings and goings without curiosity, so they said good-bye to me and the stranger and went out without a backward glance.

'Well, I'll be getting along as well,' said Archie Reede's mother. 'Good-bye, Ralph. Tell our Archie to look after himself, and that if he's any sense he'll bide where he is. There's nowt for him here.' She sighed. 'Not but what I wouldn't like to see him again. Well, good-bye, Ralph, and good luck to you.' She gathered her shawl over her shoulders. 'Thanks, Nessie,' she called from the door. 'It was grand.'

The five of us who were left settled comfortably round the fire. I still got a glow of pleasure at being accepted as one of the grown-ups. We lingered for a while, finishing our ale and talking about nothing in particular. Then a silence fell on us. I began to feel I should be glad when it was time to go.

Then the stranger stood up and went to the door of the cottage and looked out.

'I think it's about time,' he said, and Jackie nodded.

'Well, Ralph,' said Jackie, 'time to go. Benet... Benet Chertsey here—' Did his voice hesitate over the name?—'is on his way to Hexham and he's willing to take you with him. He's in a bit of a hurry; he's got to be there by morning; I've told him you'll be no bother and will keep up with him.'

Hexham, by tomorrow morning: I could be in Newcastle a few hours after that. I began to thank Benet but he interrupted me.

'Thank me when we get there,' he said, and reined my galloping hopes in to a steadier pace. 'Have you got your things together?' He certainly did not believe in wasting words.

I went to the end of the cottage, screened off by a leather curtain, where I had been sleeping each night with the children and the Royalist soldiers, who had left some days before. On to my pallet I put the few spare clothes I had. I tore one of the gold coins from its stitching in my doublet and put it into one of the socks that the woman at Blyth had given me. When Nessie found it, it would be too late for her pride to reject payment for hospitality freely given. I hoped she would understand that it was not a payment, but a sharing. Then I went back to the others and told Nessie I thought I would find it easier to keep up with Benet if I had no bundle to carry, and she did not argue with me.

Benet was looking impatient. There was no time for long farewells: a clasp of the hand and a cuff on the shoulder from Jackie and, 'Tell Madge... oh, well, never mind; she'd never understand anyway;' an encouraging nod from Cud, and a hearty kiss from Nessie, which surprised me so much that I had wiped it off with the back of my hand before I realized what I was doing. Whereupon Nessie was insulted, and my departure was a gay one after all. Then in a sudden rush, I remembered how much I owed them, Adam, and Nessie, Red Armstrong, Jackie, but I was outside before my eyes blurred.

The sun was still bright as we climbed the first hill beyond Elsdon. A figure suddenly started up out of the dry, brown heather and challenged us. Benet replied something which I did not catch but which satisfied the guard.

When we had gone about a mile farther, Benet stopped, and turned back to me.

'You know you'll have to keep up with me, don't you, lad? If you can't,' he said, 'I'll just have to leave you behind. I'm sorry, but there's more than us to think of.'

He might have said 'you', but he said 'us'. He was not as forbidding as he seemed. I told him that I would keep up with him if it killed me.

'There's another thing,' he said. 'There's one more ring of patrols to go through. So there'll be one more challenge—not long after dark. If we're stopped after that, don't wait to see what happens, just get away as quickly as you can, because the challenge won't have come from any of our men. After that, you'd have to find your own way to Newcastle.'

My elation at the idea of being back in Newcastle in a day or two had quite vanished by now. Anything might happen before I got there.

'Not that I think it's likely, but it's as well to be prepared,' Benet went on. 'If you do have to make your way on your own . . .' he paused, then said doubtfully, 'oh well, they said you were to have the tune. You'll find some as'll answer if you hum or whistle this.'

He hummed a snatch of tune which began with some false notes and some stumbling but quickly settled down into 'Down the Long Stairs'. He stopped.

'D'you know it?' he asked.

'Of course, I know it; everybody in Newcastle knows it,' I said. I did not add that to me it seemed like an omen.

'Just listen carefully,' he said; and repeated the notes again exactly as before, with the same unsteady beginning. 'You'd best mark the first bit: that's what's important.'

I whistled the notes several times, until he was satisfied.

Benet set a steady pace which did not, at first, seem difficult to keep up with. I had to walk behind him because the path was very narrow, nothing more than a sheep track. Sometimes it crossed others, or divided into two, but Benet never hesitated a moment which to take. There was sufficient light from the sun, and later from the stars for me to follow him without too much difficulty. At first the track rose steadily and then levelled out. The air was as still as it ever is on the moors and occasionally I heard rustlings in the heather, whether made by animals or human beings I could not tell. From time to time a bird called, and Benet paused and listened until the cry was repeated before going on. Once a sheep blundered suddenly out of the darkness and skittered some yards along the track before jumping into the heather, leaving me with my heart racing with fright.

I was finding Benet's pace hard to keep up with and, although the night was cold, sweat was trickling through my hair. My heart was thumping and my head was pounding, and I had forgotten the second challenge when it came. It was scarcely a challenge in the ordinary sense. Out of nowhere, an arm suddenly reached out and imprisoned my chest and arms from behind, while I was almost suffocated by the pressure of another hand on my mouth and nose. I struggled frenziedly to free myself, but whoever held me had me at a complete disadvantage and I could not.

'Go on, walk,' he said in my ear, at the same time jabbing with his knee the backs of my knees so that I almost fell.

I was half-strangled by the time I had been pushed forward some paces, off the track to what seemed to be, though by now it was well-nigh impossible to see, a cluster of large stones with a narrow space in the centre. Here I was released. I fell to my knees, too winded to try to fight. At first I could hear only my own gasping breath; then, as that grew easier, a low-voiced conversation between Benet and our attackers.

'It's all right,' said Benet. 'It's not your fault: I still don't understand why they didn't let you know I'd have the boy with me.' His voice became rueful. 'But you needn't have half-killed us before finding out who we were.'

'Who is he, anyway?' said another voice.

'Oh, I don't know: some Newcastle boy who's got to get back

by St. Luke's. Sir Adam asked me to take him. I know nowt about him; he knows nowt about me. That's the best these days.'

'Well, I suppose he's all right, if Sir Adam spoke for him,' said the voice, 'but I'm going to blindfold him. There's been too many strangers along our roads this summer: too many for safety: I don't like it.'

'All right,' said Benet, 'though for all he can see now, you might as well save yourself the trouble. But hurry up, I haven't much time to waste. There's still a good way to go before sun-up.'

My eyes were bandaged with a woollen scarf and I was led for some distance. Because of the conversation I had just heard, I took more notice of the way we were going than I would have done if I had been simply following Benet. I felt sure that we were on one of the old rievers' roads: those mysterious tracks by which the men of the hills went down into the valleys, on both sides of the Border, raided the villages, and returned to their hills as secretly as they had left them. The track, scarcely a road, was narrow and rough under foot, and was now descending rapidly. I heard the sound of water running over rocks: a fair volume of water. We had crossed the moors from Elsdon near the entrance to Redesdale, into another of the valleys of Northumberland. Since it was so well guarded, I thought it was probably Tynedale, though which part of it I had no idea.

When we reached more level ground the scarf was removed from my eyes and my escort left me with never a word.

'This is as good a place as any to stop,' said Benet. 'We'll have a drink and a bite and then it'll be straight on without stopping.'

I ate the oatcake Nessie had given me and was glad of a drink from the river, though I got my feet wet obtaining it. As we rested, Benet told me that from now on we might run into Roundhead troops. The scouts we had just left had told him that a large section of the Parliamentary army led by Cromwell himself, it was believed, was back in Northumberland from Edinburgh on its way to accept the surrender of Carlisle and might not be far from where we were.

'Whether it's true or not—and most likely it is: it's the good news that's turned out to be rumours this summer,' he said sadly, 'there's a Roundhead troop in Hexham, so we could run into a patrol anywhere now. Finished? Come on, then, I want to be in Acomb before it's light. There's something to see to there before I go on to Hexham.'

The pace he set now was more punishing than ever and left me no breath for talking or asking questions. The path seemed to be following the stream most of the time for we were never out of the sound of water: it was dropping all the time, and I discovered that it can be just as painful going downhill at a fast pace as going uphill. Breathing might be less uncomfortable but my legs began to feel so weak that I was afraid they might fail me. The fear of being abandoned by Benet kept me going, however.

At last we left the river valley and began to climb again. The darkness around us deepened; the air was more still, and it was impossible to move quietly for dry leaves crackled under our feet. Even Benet had to slow down. At last he stopped.

'We're nearly there,' he whispered. 'Wait for me here. And don't move about, mind you.' And he went off into the darkness without another word.

He need not have told me to stay still: I had no heart or energy to do anything else. It was in a wood he had left me, a fair-sized one, judging by the time we had been wading through fallen leaves. I leant against the nearest tree and settled myself to wait for his return. To a town-bred lad like me there was something frightening about a wood, even at midday: at night it was a thousand times worse. Even before I had recovered my breath and my limbs had stopped trembling, I was longing for Benet's return. I durst not whistle to keep up my spirits. Branches creaked; dead leaves rustled lightly; I strained my eyes but it was still too dark to see. Only my ears could warn me of anyone approaching. I set myself to listen: the loudest sound was my own breathing. A sudden screech made my heart stop beating, then race faster than ever. I forced myself to stay where I was; though surely a man had been murdered. Could it have been Benet? The sound died away and the wood settled into near-silence again.

I waited. Surely Benet ought to have returned by now. *Had* he been killed? Or captured? Perhaps he had never intended to return. My fear of the wood was replaced by less vague fears. Now dawn was not far off. I began to see the dim shapes of trees: then, beyond the trees a meadow. Suddenly a stealthy rustling set my heart pounding again: there was a figure coming through the wood. It did not look like Benet's. I forced myself to remain motionless. A voice, not Benet's, called softly, 'Ralph, where are you, Ralph?'

Ralph. He knew my name. It was all right. The muscles in my neck slowly unknotted. I moved forward to meet the man.

'You're coming with me, now. Something's happened: Benet's not going to Hexham.'

I knew better than to ask questions: I just mumbled, 'All right.' I was beginning to feel like a Shrove Tuesday football, kicked first by one foot, then by another but always, I hoped, a little nearer the goal. At the time it did not surprise me that there was always somebody to help me, no matter how dangerous it might be: it was years before I was detached enough from my own importance to see how amazingly lucky I had been, and how much I owed to the close-knit organization of the Borderers.

The man went on, 'We'll have to hurry: I'm behind already.'

It was growing lighter: I could see the man now. He was a weather-beaten countryman, with veined cheeks, a pointed nose, and sharp blue eyes. I was not sure that I liked what I saw.

'Here, put these on,' he said, handing me a worn homespun smock and an ancient hat. 'And I'll have your doublet in exchange. A bonnie bad bargain, too.'

I thought of the gold coin in it. I wished I had left all three at Elsdon. The man saw me hesitate.

'Come on,' he said, 'we haven't got all day. And while I think of it, Benet said that if you've got any money, you'd best hand it over to me. It'll be put to good use.'

I liked him less and less. How did I know that Benet had said that? And even if he had, why should I hand over so much money?

'I'm not going to wait here all day,' said the man. 'Be sensible, lad. You don't want to stay here by yourself, now do you? Think on; if ought went wrong and you were questioned, then mebbe searched, well, what would a farm lad be doing with money?'

I still did not trust the man, but he was right: if I were searched, gold coins would make me a highly suspicious character. Besides, I had found no use for money so far; and if he was simply charging me for his services, he was entitled to do so. I turned my back on him and managed to get one coin from its stitching. I left the one in the worn hem round the top of my breeches. When I turned round I gave the coin, together with the doublet, to the stranger. I could not bring myself to part with both coins, risky though it might be to keep any.

When the man saw that the coin was gold, his expression changed, and he stared at me curiously. He opened his lips as if to say something, but changed his mind and only turned the coin over in his hand, to feel its weight. He put it in his pocket: then he rolled up the doublet.

'This'd better be hid,' he said. 'I'll be back in a minute.'

I heard him scuffing through the leaves, but I deliberately did not look to see where he was going. I put on the old smock and hat. He soon returned and, beckoning me to follow, made for the edge of the wood. We walked about a quarter of a mile along a little lane overhung with trees to a spot where waited the thinnest and most mangy ox I had ever seen. Its patient breath steamed in the early morning air. It was harnessed to a cart loaded with hay.

The man climbed on to the cart and took the reins. He jerked his head to show that I was to jump up after him, then immediately flicked the reins and called to the ox to start, which it did but in a leisurely way fortunately, or I might have fallen.

'Are we going to Hexham?' I asked. I was sure we were, but it gave me something to say.

'Where else?' said the countryman. 'This hay's for the Roundheads there.'

'The Roundheads...' I could only repeat the words in horror.

'Aye. There was a couple of them round Acomb, Saturday, with their requisition orders for the week, damn them.' He spat viciously over the side of the shaft. 'First they take our horses, then expect us to feed them. Oh aye, they'll pay us, out of the estates of the new delinquents in these parts. But when? They haven't paid yet for all the stuff they took in '44.'

He went on grumbling about the old war and the new war and what ordinary folk had suffered from them, and ended by cursing Cavaliers and Roundheads alike with such fervour that, unnerved as I was already by the information that we were going straight to the Roundhead garrison in Hexham, I began to feel mighty uneasy and wonder to what kind of man Benet had delivered me, or even *if* Benet had handed me over.

Then he looked slyly at me and laughed. 'That's the line, Ralph, plain country folks, remember, and all we care about is to be let get on with wor own affairs. King Charles or King Parliament, what's it to us as long as they leave us be? Isn't that right, Ralph?' I did not know what to make of the man and the scowl he now gave left me more bewildered still. Then he gave me a great dig in the ribs that came at the same moment as a jolt of the cart and almost unseated me. 'Nay, Ralph, cheer up, lad. Just remember that neither of us Herons, father nor son, is ones for sticking wor shovels where there's nee muck, and you'll do fine. But just leave the talking to me. They know me well enough by now, though they've not seen my son Ralph very often.'

I began to feel vexed with the man. Why could he not say what he meant straight out, in the name of goodness, instead of talking in riddles?

'D'you mean that I have to pretend to be your son,' I asked irritably, 'and talk against both King and Parliament?'

'That's it,' he said grudgingly, 'but the less you talk the better. Benet said you were no fool.' Then his surly look became even more sour. 'Though that's more than I can say for meself, taking you on, a stranger and not even of the Old Faith.' Perhaps it was the real man at last that I saw now, looking at me with dislike. 'Don't know why I let Benet talk me into it. I'll tell you straight, the first minute any Roundhead has any suspicion of you, I'll tell him pretty quick that I don't know who you really are, and you turned up in the wood near my farm and paid me to fetch you into Hexham and put you on the road to Newcastle. That's near enough to serve. They'll believe me when I show them the gold sharp enough. Anybody that knows me will bear me out that I've never been on either side, and I've got a name for liking the feel of silver, or gold, as well as the next man.' He gave me a queer, sideways glance. 'Count yourself lucky I didn't take the lot of your money.'

I might have known that he had guessed I had kept back some of my gold. I grew more anxious than ever, and uncertain of the man's intentions.

We jolted about a mile farther along the rough road that by now had dropped to the level of a river, which I took to be the Tyne. Neither of us had anything to say. The only sounds were the grating of the wheels, the clop of the ox's hooves, the autumnal twittering of birds among dry branches and, from time to time, the swirl of the river. In spite of my anxiety, the steady motion of the cart made me drowsy—I had not slept all night—and confused, and I was struggling in a river of sleep and sinking deeper and deeper.

The cart stopped. My head jerked and jolted me back to wakefulness. We had halted just before a bridge and Roundheads were swarming round us, or so it seemed. For a confused moment I thought they had come to take me; then their questions, all addressed to Heron, and his answers made it plain that this was just a routine check of vehicles and people going into Hexham. Heron was surly and made no attempt to disguise his dislike of the troopers. What I could not understand, however, was the uneasy way that he kept on stealing glances over his shoulder at the load of hay. It made me uneasy, too, and I wondered what was wrong. I also glanced once over my shoulder, though I steeled myself not to do it again. There might be something concealed that he did not want the troopers to find, yet he was behaving in a way guaranteed to rouse suspicion. He must be a fool.

The corporal in charge had noticed our uneasiness. 'Search that hay,' he said to two of his men. I felt more nervous than ever, and Heron shifted uneasily. The corporal was in the mood for a joke. 'No, never mind,' he said. I relaxed. Then, quickly, 'Just run your swords right into it half a dozen times.' The corporal grinned at us, challengingly.

'No, no, don't do that!' yelled Heron, and he jumped down.

The corporal signed to the troopers to wait and said triumphantly, 'I thought as much. What—or who—have you got hidden in that hay, you son of Belial?'

The owner of the cart did not reply. He hobbled to the back of the cart, in his anxiety pushing the troopers unceremoniously aside. We were all watching him intently. He carefully removed some of the hay, then another layer, and another. Then, from my seat on the cart, I could see, nestling in the hay, each neatly wrapped in straw, about a dozen small round objects: nothing more or less dangerous than—eggs. It was a second before anyone moved. Then one of the troopers started to laugh, a great guffaw that he strangled in mid-career when he saw his corporal's face, a furious blend of disappointment and anger.

The corporal did his best. 'See what else there is,' he said, to the troopers; then to Heron, 'Trying to smuggle them into Hexham, of course. When the requisitioning officers come round, the hens are never laying, are they?'

The owner of the cart looked stupidly round at the troops, then back at the corporal. 'Oh, no, sir,' he said. 'Present for the Captain, sir. Just wanted to be sure they'd get to him safe.'

As he took in the implications of the man's words, the corporal's speech deserted him, and before he recovered it, Heron turned to the cart again, and feeling in the hay, he produced a small shank of bacon. He shook off the bits of hay sticking to it, and said to the corporal meaningly, 'This was for the Captain as well, but what the eye never sees the heart never grieves over and, anyway, the Captain's a good man for looking out for his men. He'd be glad to think you and the lads'd had a taste of meat for once,' and he held the meat out towards the corporal. The corporal looked at it, licked the corner of his mouth, hesitated, then suddenly roared, 'Tempter, Satan,' and knocked it out of the man's hand.

A further search of the cart produced a fair-sized cube of butter wrapped in wet cloths, and a small side of bacon. The corporal was angry, feeling tricked, for he had expected to find some miserable Royalist hiding in the cart, but the countryman was breaking no law, so all the corporal could do was to take the man's name and the name of his farm and utter vague threats about what would happen if the food supplies were not delivered to the Roundhead garrison, since the man had sworn that that was where he was taking them.

Apparently unmoved, Heron clambered back beside me on the cart, gave the signal to the ox, and we lumbered across the bridge, I not daring to turn round to see if the troopers were watching our departure, and Heron not caring.

'Reckon I ought to make you pay for them eggs and meat,' said Heron, when we were safely over the bridge. 'Could have got a good price for them off auld Luck, the innkeeper. Now they'll have to be wasted on cursed Parliament men: they could make things awkward for a poor farmer, if they wanted to turn nasty.' Then he sniffed contemptuously. 'Trust them to catch the sprat and miss the mackerel. Just as well for you.' In spite of his grumbling, he was in a good humour because of the success of his scheme for distracting attention away from me, for he gave me a ferocious but friendly dig with his sharp elbow. 'Got you to Hexham, like I said, didn't I?'

I agreed, my distrust of him now gone, and I tried to thank him, but he scarcely listened. We were in the town now, rattling and bumping over the cobbles. He shouted to the ox, pulled on the reins, then turned to me.

'All right, you can get off now. Nay, there's no need to look so gormless. I said I'd fetch you into Hexham, and into Hexham I've fetched you. You can shift for yourself now. Come on, hurry up, afore folks start to stare,' he said.

This last admonition was unnecessary: there was nobody to stare—the street was deserted. I climbed down too dismayed to say a word. He cracked his whip at his ancient beast, which slithered on the cobbles in its efforts to start the heavy cart; then he gave a quick glance around, and apparently softening, bent down a little and whispered, 'You've got the tune: try the "White Horse".' At least that's what I thought he said. The clatter of hooves and wheels drowned anything else, if indeed anything else were said.

For the first time since I had met Kit and Archie I was really on my own, with no one to tell me what to do. I had only the notes of a tune and the name of an inn—the 'White Horse' had to be the name of an inn—to help me through a Roundhead-occupied town, along a busy road and into Newcastle, the chief Roundhead centre in the whole of the North. However, I reminded myself that I had reached Hexham safely, that my own family might by now be looking out for me, and that I could walk to Newcastle in a few hours. But before I started to do that I might at least try my luck at the 'White Horse'.

Chapter 18

Hexham is not a large town, and it was not long before I came to the market-place. When I entered it I understood why the rest of the town had been so deserted: most of the townspeople must have been in the square. A cordon of soldiers kept the crowd back from the centre of the square, and also kept open a way to the arch of the tower-house which was at the far end. I could see at once that I had come upon a Roundhead cere-monial punishment day, familiar enough in Newcastle but apparently a novelty to the people of Hexham. In the centre of the square were the wooden horse, the punishment stools, and two whipping posts. The court-martial could not have been long in progress for only the punishment stools were occupied.

Almost as I joined the edge of the crowd a murmur of excite-ment rippled round it, and every head turned towards the archway in the tower-house. Another prisoner was being escorted through the arch. The excitement died quickly away: only another minor offender; with hands tied behind his back, and cleft stick on his tongue, he was led through the square and a way cleared through the spectators. His offence must have been swearing, and he was being led to expiate his crime on a punishment stool, not in the square this time, but elsewhere, probably outside the tavern where it had been committed.

He was quickly followed by two other soldiers, who must have been convicted of plundering or offering violence to civilians, for they were tied up, so that they stood on tiptoe, and then the lashing began. By the time it stopped, neither of the prisoners was conscious. As far as I could tell from the com-ments of the people round me, no sympathy was being wasted on the men: the punishment was richly deserved.

'A body wouldn't feel safe in his bed, else,' said a solemn-faced man just in front of me, a tradesman, by his comfortable dress, and his neighbours murmured agreement.

I could not see very well from my position on the fringe of the crowd and tried to wriggle my way forward. I might have done much better to slip away through the town while everyone was so occupied, but I think I was so engrossed in the spectacle that I forgot my own predicament. A comfortable-looking country-woman gave me a friendly push forward and said, in a loud voice, 'Let the lad through,' and it seemed that every head turned to look at me and I cursed myself for being so stupid. The solemn-faced tradesman muttered something about 'a pretty big lad', but no one backed him up and I was pushed to the front of the crowd into a fine position where I could see between the shoulders of two of the cordon of troopers.

I tried to make myself as inconspicuous as possible but my neighbours scarcely noticed me, for the next prisoner had just appeared and was being hoisted on to the wooden horse, poor devil. What he had done I knew not, but by the time he was taken down he would have been well and truly punished.

So far the crowd had enjoyed their unusual entertainment, though in a quiet enough way: Roundhead soldiers were not popular in Northumberland. There was a break in the flow of prisoners from the tower-house, but there must be more to come because all the people still waited. Then, at last, three more prisoners came through the archway. They were different from the earlier prisoners: these were no common soldiers, but gentlemen, by their dress, and that was surely Langdale's colours they were wearing. They were escorted by a group of Roundhead officers. I caught sight of a chaplain among them. No wonder the watching throng gasped.

'Never thought they'd dare,' breathed a voice behind me.

'Whisht, man,' said his neighbour.

The three prisoners were halted so that they stood facing the centre of the market square, and a foot or two in front of their escort. The chaplain detached himself from the escort. He stood somewhat to one side of the prisoners so that both they and the crowd could see him. (The Roundheads always made as much of a show as possible of their punishment ceremonies.) He spoke to the three men—it was impossible to catch his words—then stretched out his hand, palm upward. On it lay three pieces of paper, neatly folded.

One officer seemed to be in charge of the proceedings. He spoke to the three prisoners: then he spoke to each in turn; each shook his head and gazed steadfastly in front of him, ignoring the chaplain's outstretched hand. By now it was clear what was happening. All three men had been sentenced to death, but not all were to die. The chaplain was holding out lots for each to choose his own destiny. It was strange that they all refused to choose, as if they all rejected the justice of their sentence and would have no part in such mercy.

Then the officer in charge must have raised his voice for now we heard him say, 'Your crime has been against the people of England and their duly elected Parliament. Let the people decide among you.' He turned and cried out to us, 'Let one of you assembled here to see justice done come forward.'

No one stirred. He summoned a soldier from the cordon. The man went forward to receive his order, then marched back to the gap he had left in the cordon and pushed into the crowd. He stopped at a man with a small child perched on his shoulders. He lifted up his arms and made to take the child, who whimpered and clung more closely to his father.

'It's all right,' said the soldier in a soothing voice. 'I won't hurt you. There's no call to be scared. Just come and do what the man says, and see what he'll give you.'

'Nay, it's not a bairn's work,' said the father, making no move to hand the child down.

' 'Tis the Lord's work,' said the trooper, and he lifted the boy from his father's shoulders. The father clutched the boy for a second.

'You'd best let him,' said the trooper, 'or you'll answer for it.'

The man slowly withdrew his hands.

'Don't be scared, son,' he said. 'I'm here waiting for you.'

We had all watched as if in a trance. There was not a murmur from the crowd. The child was taken to the chaplain, who bent down and told him what to do. He was bewildered and a little frightened. He looked towards his father, who had been brought to the edge of the cordon. His father nodded reassurance and the little boy stretched up his hand and took one of the pieces of paper from the chaplain's outstretched hand. The chaplain leant down again, said something to the child and gestured towards the three prisoners, who stared, unmoving, straight ahead of them. The child went towards the prisoners and stopped in front of them. I drew my breath and my muscles went tight. The little boy looked at the condemned men, hesitated, then offered the paper to the man in the middle. The man did not look at or put out his hand to receive the lot. The child could not understand: he went closer, raised himself on tiptoe and beat the man with the paper, to make him take it. The man remained motionless, eyes still fixed straight ahead. The child turned round to see what he must do. The officer in charge came and took the paper, opened it and read in a loud voice for all to hear, 'Life given by God'. The crowd stirred but the reprieved man did not move. The officer took his arm and drew him away from the other two. He moved as if his limbs were lead.

Then the child went back to the chaplain and took a second lot. He knew what to do this time and scarcely hesitated before holding out his hand to the taller of the two prisoners. Again it was the officer in charge who had to take the lot. Even he could not remain unmoved: his voice trembled a little and then steadied itself as he read, 'Life given by God.'

A rustle of sound passed through the square. A woman screamed and broke into wild sobs. The condemned man, now standing alone, moved for the first time. He turned his head in the direction of the sobbing: a tremor passed over his face. That was all.

The thing was soon over: the escort moving in; the chaplain lifting his voice in prayer; the group shuffling back through the arch of the tower; then, finally the shots and the rolling of the drum; the furtive sign of the cross from a woman at my elbow; and, last of all, the voice of the officer in charge crying out over the square that this was the punishment legally decreed for all revolters from Parliament.

It was a terrible reminder that Parliament was carrying out its threat to regard as traitors all who had changed sides in this new war. Would the next step be to condemn to death even those who had fought only for their king from the beginning of the troubles? I was one of them; what was I doing in that crowd? I must have been mad to linger there. Yet I durst not try to slip away now. I must wait until the people began to disperse.

What were they all waiting for? There was muttering among the crowd. It grew louder, then a voice called out to the officer and soldiers still on duty in front of the tower, 'What about the others? What about my bairn; what are you going to do to him?'

The question was taken up: others in that gathering had husbands and sons Royalist prisoners there. The pressure on the cordon was steadily increasing and slowly the soldiers were forced back. The space in the middle of the square began to crumple. The soldiers in front of the tower had dressed their pikes, and waited motionless for further orders. Then a door in the tower, which I had not noticed before, opened, and two men came out. The first, a sergeant, called for silence, but he used his breath needlessly, for the crowd had begun to quieten the moment he was noticed. The second, an officer, stepped to the front of the little platform in front of the door, and unrolling a scroll, began to read. The officers of the Hexham garrison in court-martial had, that day, found guilty of taking part in the late risings in the North, the following. Here came a list of, I suppose, sixty or so names. Some of the names were foreign to these parts, mostly Scottish names, presumably of men who had escaped capture at Preston but had been taken as they were straggling home. Such names aroused no response from the listeners. More numerous were good Northumbrian names: Crisp, Fenwick, Luck, Neale, Heron. When one of the names was read out, a man's harsh voice screamed, 'You cannut, you cannut. He's nowt but a silly bairn.' The reader did not falter, but read on to the end of the names.

The officer paused, then went on reading; 'Propositions having been received from diverse merchants of the City of Newcastle by the Committee lately appointed by Parliament for the transportation of prisoners for foreign service, the same having been accepted, the said merchants giving security to transport them thither, and that they shall not return, the above-named prisoners are hereby sentenced to be disposed of for Venice, the said merchants and contractors to discharge their obligation within fourteen days of this eighteenth day of October in the one thousand six hundred and forty eighth year of our Lord.'

He handed the proclamation to the sergeant to be posted where all could see it, but those most nearly concerned had already heard the names they waited for.

There was nothing in the proclamation that I wanted to study more closely and for the first time my attention wandered away from the tower-house and the space in front of it. The close-packed crowd had not begun to move yet: the people were angry and unwilling to leave. But they were helpless against Parliament, and knew it. Then at last, though still with sullen looks, they began to move and I could move too. As I had waited, I had had time to look at the buildings round the market-place and I had noticed that there was an inn adjacent to the tower-house. I had glanced at its sign idly enough at first: I did not really expect the 'White Horse' to be a prosperous inn in the main square: it seemed much more likely to be a little ale-house in a side alley. Yet the painted board surely showed a deal of white. As the crowd was now beginning to thin out, I edged my way near enough to the inn to see the sign clearly. It *was* the 'White Horse'. What was I to do? In my shabby smock and battered hat, I could scarcely walk straight into such a prosperous inn.

Trying to look like a country lad with time on his hands, I wandered across to the middle of the market-place to stare at the Roundheads doing penance there. They had been forgotten temporarily in the more terrible punishments of Royalists that had just been proclaimed, but the two men on the punishment stools and the man on the wooden horse were still there. Some town louts were now standing and shouting taunts, while more sober citizens, in twos and threes, were trying to read the placards on the men's backs, to see what crimes they had committed.

As I stood and gaped, I was trying to decide how to get into the 'White Horse' without attracting attention to myself. Out of the corner of my eye I noticed that a small group was gathering in front of the tower-house gate. Still in my part of country lad with time to spare before returning to his village, I strolled back to see what was happening. It was simply a crowd of patient people waiting, and staring at the gate. They were not idle sightseers. I noticed an old farmer and his wife, who was weeping quietly and hopelessly. The old man held her hand and gently patted it, while neither said a word, but gazed at the gate as if they durst not turn their eyes away. Their grief and their air of hopeless waiting was mirrored in the others there. I guessed that they were waiting for the Royalist prisoners named in the proclamation, in case they were marched away tonight, hoping to catch a last glimpse of a son, a husband, a brother.

It scarcely seemed decent to stay with them. Deciding that now was the moment to risk entering the stable-yard of the 'White Horse' when there were a number of idle sightseers about the square, of whom I might well be one, I had half turned away when I felt a stir in the small crowd. The gate of the tower-house had been unlocked by a soldier inside; the corporal in charge of the guard shouted orders and the guard opened its ranks to allow three men to pass through. The three men were not soldiers, but well-dressed, sober citizens. Of course, the 'diverse merchants of Newcastle'.

And one of them was Thomas Trumbell.

Chapter 19

My first feeling was of relief: the Borderers had succeeded in getting a message through to my mother. Then doubt followed almost immediately. Thomas Trumbell was trusted by the Parliament men in Newcastle: he must be, or he would not be allowed a share in the profitable business of selling their enemies. Could I trust him, or ought I to slip away from the group round him as inconspicuously as possible before he saw me? I stood undecided. The wife of the old man had stopped crying and was clutching Thomas Trumbell's cloak. All three merchants were surrounded by men and women clamouring to know when the Royalist prisoners would leave Hexham, or begging to be allowed to see them to say farewell.

The merchants were unmoved, save by vexation, and Thomas Trumbell, unable to free himself, turned to the sentries still standing in front of the gate and called for help. Then his voice faltered, then recovered: I doubt whether anyone else noticed it. I knew what had happened. It was too late for me to run away now; he had recognized me. I looked at him: he stared straight into my eyes for a brief second.

'Corporal,' he called, 'order two of your men to escort us through this mob to the "White Horse".'

The corporal was embarrassed. 'I cannot do that, sir, without orders.'

'Orders, orders,' another of the merchants spoke. 'This *is* an order.'

'Sorry, sir,' said the corporal. 'We cannot leave the gate without orders.'

I took advantage of the argument that followed to move away from the crowd, which was growing as other people in the market-place became aware of what was happening, and made, not for the main entrance to the 'White Horse', but for the arch that must surely lead to the stable-yard. I felt sure that Thomas Trumbell had named the inn deliberately, to let me know where to get in touch with him. I still did not entirely trust him, but he could have denounced me the moment he set eyes on me. Besides, I had no plan of my own for reaching home.

I strolled through the inn archway, still like a country lad exploring the town—or so I hoped. The stable-yard was empty. I hesitated, then—I could think of nothing else to do—I whistled the rievers' tune. At once a short, wrinkled old ostler came out of one of the stables.

'What do you want? What are you doing here?' he asked.

'Have you any work?' I asked, on the spur of the moment. Under my breath I added, 'A word with Master Trumbell'. I raised my voice again. 'I'm used to horses.'

'You'll have to see the gaffer,' he said snappishly. 'I don't hire the hands. But you can save yourself the trouble. He's paying folk off, not taking fresh ones on. So get yourself off the way you came.' All this was said in a loud voice and with warning grimaces and jerks of the head in the direction of the stable out of which he had come. Then after a quick look round the yard, he came nearer and hissed, 'The hay-loft at the end: be sharp.' He turned back into the stable with noisy grumblings about being fetched away from his work by idle good-for-nothings. 'Got rid of him pretty sharp, though,' was the last thing I heard him say as I raced as quietly as I could along the yard and up the stone steps outside what was obviously the hay-loft, praying that no one would come into the yard either from the street or from the inn.

The hay was warm and soft in the dim corner where I settled down to wait. I was tired. My hot eyes kept on closing. I had had no rest the night before. I fell asleep.

Someone was shaking me, roughly. A hand, smelling of the stables, was clamped over my mouth. I was startled awake and struggled to free myself. A voice hissed in my ear, 'It's all right. Be quiet. Understand?' I nodded. The hand was removed. It was now quite dark in the loft. By the light of an old horn lamp I could see that it was the ostler who spoke. There was another figure casting shadows also; not, as I half expected, Thomas Trumbell, but a young man, about my own age and size. I had seen men like him at Elsdon, and, for that matter, in Newcastle a year or two before. He was a Scotsman, by his dress a northern Scot.

'Now listen and don't interrupt,' said the ostler, 'for there's not much time. You're to change places with this Sawney here. He's one of them lot that's to be transported. Nay, don't

163

interrupt, you'll catch on in a minute. You're to wear his clothes and take his place in the jail tonight. Sunrise tomorrow all the prisoners are being marched to Newcastle to wait shipment to Venice. You'll be among them. Come on, change clothes with him; we've got to get you into the jail as fast as may be.'

The ostler seemed to think this explanation enough, and the Scot, who obviously knew what he had to do, nodded encouragingly at me. But I prepared to make a fight of it. I could see Thomas Trumbell's game. I was not going to submit tamely to being forced into jail in place of a red-shanked Scot. I had come too far and was too near home for that, even if they *were* two to one.

'Hurry up,' said the ostler, as I made no move. 'You've got to be in the jail in a few minutes, before the sentries change, or the whole thing'll fall through.'

'Look,' I said, trying to keep my voice down, 'if I'd wanted to go to the galleys I could have given myself up any time in the last two months. You must think I'm daft.'

'Don't be a fool,' said the ostler. 'You wanted a word with Thomas Trumbell, didn't you? Well, this is all his idea, and a pretty penny it's costing him. Parliament soldiers don't bribe cheap, you know. You don't think I give a groat what happens to you, d'you, even if you have got the tune? I don't know who you are—and I don't want to know—nor what you are to a Parliament man like Master Trumbell, that he should spend good money and stick his neck out for you. But I'm not sticking mine out any farther, so you can get out of here, quick, whether it's with me you go or not.'

'Just a minute,' I said, 'how do I know this is Master Trumbell's plan? I felt I must placate him now. 'The whole scheme sounds crazy. You can't blame me for being careful, now can you?'

'Oh, aye. Trumbell said to say to you, "The King's ring", that'd show you,' said the ostler.

The King's ring; the ring given to my father by King Charles the night I was born was always called that. I was convinced: the ostler could not possibly have known about the ring.

Why didn't you mention it straight off? I thought, but I only said, 'Right. That's good enough.'

Quickly the Scot and I changed clothes. I do not know that

he made a good farm lad: there was something too proud and untamed in his bearing. I had never thought to appear as a Scot, but the clothes were distinctive—blue woollen waistcoat, bases of plaid, stockings of the same, and a pair of worn pumps—and an Englishman at least would look at the dress more than at the youth wearing it. The Scot took the cloak from my right shoulder and, murmuring words I did not understand, flung it over my left shoulder. He looked at me, then down at himself—distastefully. Then he clasped my hand and shook it. Then, struggling for English words, 'Thank you. You have been lucky for me. A good journey's ending,' he said.

The ostler was impatient with such niceties. 'You know what you have to do?' he said. The Scot nodded. 'Right then. Give us time to get into the street.' The ostler spoke slowly, as to a dull child. He turned to me. 'Come on and, remember, say nowt from now on. Just follow.'

He took me out of the inn yard by a backdoor that led into a quiet lane. There was just enough moonlight for me to follow without stumbling on the unfamiliar cobbles. We stopped in front of a small iron-studded door, the only opening in a tall stone wall: it must have been a lesser entrance to the tower-house. The ostler beat a light, patterned knock on the door. As soon as he heard oiled bolts sliding back, the man turned and slipped back into the shadows of the lane. The door opened a little, a hand appeared and beckoned me in. I slipped through the opening. A man in Roundhead uniform whispered, 'Come with me,' and led me along a stone-flagged passage, unlocked a door, and then pitched me into a dark room, saying threateningly, 'Mebbe you'll be quiet in there, you cursed Scot, where there's nobody can talk your own gibberish to you.'

The push he gave me sent me stumbling over bodies stretched out on the floor, and there was a spate of startled curses, followed by questions. I did not reply except in a kind of gibberish, which came to me out of nowhere, or perhaps from my schooldays when Emmet and I used to torment Alyse by talking to her in a language of our own which was partly bits of Latin and Greek which I had passed on to Emmet, who would have liked to go to school herself, and partly made-up words of our own—the sort of thing that many children delight in at some time or other. The prisoners—for such I supposed these men to be—grumbled a little while about having a Highlander put among decent folk, though one voice spoke up and said that they were all in the same boat and might have worse companions before long, and they'd better not be so choosey. Soon the chuntering died down, snores took the place of voices, and I was the only one left awake.

I had slept part of the day, in the hay-loft, so I was only half-tired now: not tired enough to go to sleep: too tired to keep my fears reasonable. So I spent most of the night afraid that Thomas Trumbell had found a perfect way of disposing of an unwanted stepson: that my mother might never see me again; afraid of what she would say, if we did meet again; afraid of the months ahead (I did not realize they would be *years* not months) that I must spend out of England. Even if Thomas Trumbell were playing fair, I could see only exile ahead. It is small wonder that when I did finally fall asleep, my sleep was tormented again by a dream that I had had more than once since Tynemouth, in which I was trying to escape from Harbottle Grimston and running down the Long Stairs, but no matter how many stairs I leapt down, there were always more and I never reached the Close.

Chapter 20

The late afternoon sun was doing its best to soften the grim stones when at last we shuffled to a halt ouside the West Gate of Newcastle, but the walls, which never hitherto had offered me anything but shelter and protection, now seemed to hold a threat or, at best, a question.

We had been bawled and kicked awake before dawn, manacled together in fours and lined up outside the tower-house in Hexham. The duty officer of the garrison had satisfied himself that the number of prisoners was correct, and handed us over to the Newcastle merchants. It had been considered necessary to provide only six troopers on horseback to escort us to Newcastle, shackled and half-starved as we were. Yet, weak though we were, we had been forced to keep up a gruelling pace: the road between Hexham and Newcastle was a good one and there was a tradition of travelling fast in the Parliament army. No rations had been provided; the garrison quartermaster was wasting no provisions on us: we were now the responsibility of the merchants who had bought us. We would be fed when we got to Newcastle.

The formalities of our entrance into the city were soon over. The guards on the West Gate knew Thomas Trumbell and the other merchants. Their passes were in order, and the papers for their prisoners. We were quickly counted, once by a sergeant, a second time by an officer. Neither so much as glanced at our faces.

I was one of twenty counted off from the others to be kept in the West Gate itself. The rest were marched off along Westgate Road to the Castle which was where they were to be imprisoned. Six of us were taken through the gatehouse, through the guardroom above, and eventually to a small, gloomy cell which I felt must be in the city wall itself. The guards took off our manacles, but the relief from their painful chafing was all we got that night. In spite of appeals to the guards who led us to the cell, no food appeared, not even a draught of water.

The miserable hours dragged the night away. We were too tired and too dispirited for much talk. I gave up all pretence of not understanding English, but no one seemed surprised or even interested. Each man was too sunk in his own despair to wonder about another's affairs. Black doubt swept over me. I had indeed returned to Newcastle during St. Luke's Fair, but what use was that? I was a prisoner. Not a look or a word had Thomas Trumbell given me since the night before outside the 'White Horse'. He had not come near me during the march to Newcastle. And how could he help me to escape from this place? Could I be sure that he wanted my escape?

I began to see that I had been nicely tricked into being transported without even a trial, so that I would disappear without a trace. Thomas Trumbell had made his plans carefully. He was obviously known to the Roundheads as a merchant who dealt in prisoners, though he had not been doing this when I left home. It could be coincidence that he had found me. More probably he, together with his partners, whoever they were, bought all the Royalist soldiers captured in the North, so that if I were caught I was certain to fall into his hands and be prettily disposed of to the plantations or to the Venetian galleys —it did not matter which: no one was likely to return from either—and he could take over the Cole ventures with no inconvenient stepson in the way. If I had wanted to make him a present of my inheritance I could scarcely have set about it in a better way. As time went by my mother would be persuaded that I had perished: at last even loyal Emmet would forget me.

The weary night passed. When I awoke, cold and aching from an uncomfortable half sleep, grey light was seeping through the narrow, barred slit in the wall. The man on my right was already awake, and staring apathetically in front of him. The young man on the other side was muttering in his sleep and was not far from waking. Sounds coming through the narrow window suggested that outside day had begun for the men on the West Gate and for the country people bringing their produce to dispose of in the Newcastle markets. I could hear the creaking of cart wheels, the men shouting to their horses; voices raised in disgust over the tolls just paid to the city toll collectors. It was all so homely, and I was as far away from it as if I were already in Venice: I felt the tears come to my eyes. Afraid they might spill over and shame me, I got up, picked my way over my fellow prisoners, and stood close to the window slit. The sounds grew a little clearer, but I could see nothing. Our prison must be on the town side of the West Gate, judging by the sounds. That was all I found out, but at least my tears were checked. Other prisoners were now behind me, wanting to listen and to breathe the fresh air, so I gave way to them and went back to my place by the wall.

A key groped in the lock: we all turned to the door. Two jailers came in with food and drink at last: only barley bread, hard cheese, and water, but they tasted very good. The jailers were friendly enough: one was disposed to talk and give us news. Lieutenant-General Cromwell was now said to be in Carlisle. He and Sir Arthur Hazelrigg had left Edinburgh and had marched part of the way south together, but had then separated, Cromwell going to Carlisle and Sir Arthur back to Newcastle. Sir Athur had been at the great feast of the Mayor's last night before he went on to Durham and then to Barnard Castle, where there was to be a great meeting of the gentlemen of the four northern counties to settle the affairs of the North. Newcastle had just now petitioned Parliament for the speeding up of justice against the delinquents so that their estates could be sold and Parliament's armies paid.

'There's plans for putting down the mosstroopers,' said the talkative jailer, 'and for rounding up Royalists that have returned to their homes, intending, they do say, to hatch new plots this winter.' The man talked as if he had no idea that all his wretched prisoners were Royalists. He rambled on: it was hard to know how much of his news would be correct. Then he said something which made my heart leap: 'Major-General Skippon's regiment that's been so long in Newcastle yesterday morning marched to Durham.' If there were still officers billeted at home in the Close they would be new ones who did not know me. In spite of my gloomy doubts about Thomas Trumbell, part of me still hoped I might get home again.

Everyone was suddenly more cheerful and we talked as we ate our stale bread and cheese.

'Fattening us up to get a good price for us in Venice,' said one man, but his joke was not very well received.

One prisoner, a man in his middle twenties, perhaps the oldest of us, thought that as the war seemed really to be over, the King might already have come to terms with Parliament and we might yet be saved from being sent to Venice.

'Nay,' said another, 'Parliament'll see that it doesn't come to terms until it's got shot of anybody that could fight again.'

We all felt this to be true and our cheerfulness soon died. The young man who had slept next to me and who had seemed too deep in misery to join in any talk, now spoke for the first time.

'D'you think,' he asked, 'they'll let anybody come and see us before we go?' His poor voice trembled.

There was a moment's pause, then the oldest man said, 'They might: it all depends. Has your folk any money? The jailers and guards usually make a bit when they can.'

The lad shook his head. 'Nay, they've nought but what they grow, and there's not often enough of that to spare to take to market to make any brass.'

'Nay, lad, they're the lucky ones these days. They might manage summat with a few eggs or a piece of meat. You can't eat silver, nor gold neither, though mebbe there's some as'll be wishing they could before they're much older, the way things is shaping,' said the older man. He reflected, then went on, 'Mebbe we'll be the lucky ones, after all. Whoever buys us in Venice will surely want to keep his investment alive. Like the coal-owners feed their horses in bad times, though the men can go starve.'

I thought of the man I had gone to the salt-pans to pay off, the day when I had joined the Royalists in Tynemouth. All the same, I would rather have been in his place than in the West Gate jail waiting to be transported. So would the other prisoners, I think: there was no enthusiasm in their replies to the speaker's bitter optimism. In half-hearted conversation we passed some time away: I could not say how much, for it is difficult to measure the passing of time when all its landmarks have gone.

Then again the key scraped in the lock and the heavy door was pushed open. A man came in. 'Only five minutes, mind you,' said the jailer, and he withdrew, locking us in again.

I leapt to my feet and yelled, 'Archie!' Warm hope flooded through my veins; then ebbed again. 'You're not a prisoner as well, are you?'

'No, no, man,' said Archie. 'They gave me a permit to come and see you, my own brother; your boat's sailing for London, then Venice, tomorrow.'

Then he moved forward, as far away from the door as he

could get and beckoned us to come close to him.

'Now listen,' he said, 'we've only got five minutes. Keep an ear on the door, will you?' he asked the optimistic man, who nodded and moved towards it without question. Archie quickly, unhooked his doublet, slipped it off, and pulled his thick shirt over his head. 'Come on, lad. Don't stand there gawping, give us a hand.' He started to unwrap long strips of coarse linen which were wound round his body. 'Better than rope,' he said, 'can't be felt just by touching: ropes might. Wish I'd taken a chance, though; the careless beggar didn't even touch me. Now wrap that round yourself,' he said to me, 'while I talk. Listen, all of you. I warrant you'd all like a shot at getting out of here. The window's no good: you'd never get that bar broken without a file and I couldn't risk trying to get one past the guard. Take too long, anyway; and make too much noise. And you might be seen from outside.' We were all listening hard. 'There's only one way.' A secret passage, I thought at once: this part of the town where the monasteries used to be was said to be riddled with underground passages. But even as I thought this, Archie was going on: 'You'll have to let yourselves down through the *garde-robe* there. It's not very far down, and it comes down into a chute into a ditch *inside* the town walls. The chute opening was damaged during the siege and has never been repaired, so you'll have no trouble getting out. Once you're out, the rest's up to you. There's only one thing'— everyone looked at him expectantly and a little fearfully— 'give the lad first go. It's his folk that've worked this out. They've been watching for him for weeks now.'

The other prisoners looked at me, then at each other, and nodded acceptance of the bargain. The man at the door gave a warning hiss. Archie was speaking rapidly now. 'Wait till it's dark and the West Gate's shut for the night. Remember there'll be a guard on the wall: keep quiet until you're well away from the walls. And you,' he was avoiding using my name, 'I'll be waiting for you, but if anything stops me, you'll know where to make for?' I nodded: there was only one place I could go to. 'All right: just go canny and it'll all go as sweetly as a marriage bell.' The man listening at the door had come back to his own place, the other prisoners moved away from Archie and me. Archie grabbed me and embraced me. 'Look upset, lad; we're saying good-bye, mebbe for ever.' For a moment I did not realize what he meant. The jailer was coming in again. Archie kissed me, and turned away, saying good-bye in a gruff voice; then went out with the jailer.

'Well,' said the optimistic man, 'I don't know who you are; no, I don't want to know: but it was a stroke of luck for us to be put in with you, and no mistake, wasn't it, lads?'

The others agreed, but there was now some constraint in their attitude towards me. I was somehow separated from them: I must be 'somebody'. We did not talk very much, partly from fear of being overheard, and partly because each of us was busy with his own thoughts and plans.

I found myself living again the last two months. Sometimes it was a place that slid into my mind, but more often a face: Ambrose Grimston and the brother who had killed him. As I looked in my mind at the face of Harbottle Grimston, I saw now more clearly than at Cartington that he would never again be the same assured man I had once known. I saw again the dark Presbyterian; and the corporal at Hexham. Most of all it was of my friends that I thought: the Daggs at Cullercoats; the widow at Blyth whose gift I had despised; rough, kind Nessie; Archie, who was so sure I was one of the lucky ones and did not begrudge me my luck; the new Jackie of Elsdon, the old Jackie of Tynemouth: all the simple, humble people I would once have thought scarcely worthy of the notice of Ralph Cole. And Thomas Trumbell, whom I had only now accepted as an honest man—more than honest, a generous man: I was not of his party, but he was risking his hopes for the future to help me. And Adam, always Adam, patient and strong, who had helped me though I was not of his faith, and who had taught me more than he knew. I could never repay any of them, only through others.

Time limped by. The jailers came and brought us another meal: I suppose it would be about sunset. The talkative jailer told us that we were to be put on board ship next morning and were to sail with the afternoon tide. He even knew the name of the ship—I can still remember it— the *Good Fortune*. Before Archie's visit the name would have seemed a cruel joke, now I took it as a good omen.

After they had locked us in again for the night we settled ourselves for the last stretch of waiting. The other prisoners had long since decided the order in which they would make their escape. There was little to talk about. At last we heard through the narrow window slit the sounds of the guard changing for the night watch. We waited until quiet settled on the gatehouse; then waited again. Finally, the optimistic man touched my arm. We both got up. He moved towards the door and took up a listening position. We all knew what we had to do. I pulled off my shirt and, as fast as my fingers would let me, unwound the strips of linen that Archie had brought. Another of the prisoners, who had been a seaman and said he could handle ropes in his sleep, never mind the dark, twisted the linen into a rope, painfully short, surprisingly strong.

I took one end of the rope: the seaman and another of the prisoners held the other. I had thought I was calm but my heart was beating fast and my breathing was hard. They braced themselves to take the strain of my weight, and I lowered myself into the narrow, noisome cavity. I jerked down the black, slimy pit, hung for a second, then forced myself to let go and dropped—it was not far after all—into a soft, stinking ooze.

It was not difficult to find the place where the chute came out into the ditch, for stones had been removed to make the opening bigger. I stumbled out, kicking rubble as I fumbled my way over broken masonry: it was lucky for me that Parliament had not had money to spare for the walls to be repaired after the siege. Afraid that a sentry on the wall might have heard me, I waited for a few seconds before slipping quickly into the shadow of the nearest building. A hand grasped my arm. It was Archie, waiting for me as he had promised.

'Let's get away from here as sharp as we can,' he said. 'Now, remember, if we *should* meet any curious body, you've had a drop too much, and tumbled into the laystall.' The anxiety in his voice was lightened by amusement for a moment. 'That'd not be hard to credit. Your clothes speak for themselves. But, with a bit of luck—and you're a lucky one, Ralph, I've always said it—nobody'll stop us.'

He took my arm and we set off, quickly at first, but slowing to an erratic, staggering pace as we came nearer the middle of the town. There were scarcely half a dozen people abroad, and they were too intent on getting to their beds to worry about us. We passed my old school, and turned down Tuthill Gate, catching a glimpse of the Castle where its mass showed a blackness more solid than elsewhere, and at last came to the head of

Tuthill Steps. As we went, Archie had been explaining what arrangements had been made for getting me safely into the house in the Close, where Roundhead officers were still billeted, though not Harbottle Grimston—'Summat's changed him, they say,' he said—and what I must do. Now Archie stopped and said in a low voice, 'This is where I leave you, Ralph,' and he flung his arms round my shoulders in a mock drunken embrace and muttered, 'Good luck, lad, you're nearly home,' and disappeared.

The Tuthill Steps were not as familiar to me as the Long Stairs, which I had used every day on my way home from school, but which Archie had said were too near the Castle for me to take now. Down the steep steps I went, cautiously, for they were in deep shadow from the houses that walled them in. I had to stop for breath—I was so excited and nervous—about half-way down, where the steps took a slight turn. I went on; at last the steps came to an end: I almost fell, expecting one more and not finding it. The darkness was less solid now. I could see the Mansion House across the street. Its windows were unlit: it was fortunate that it was last night that the Mayor had entertained Hazelrigg, and not tonight.

I was in the Close now, every cobble familiar to my feet. I hugged the deepest shadows of the house. Soon there would be no shadows to hide me. Now the dangerous moment was here: I was almost home. There were lights in the windows of the Great Chamber above the counting-house and the entrance. A burst of laughter and the sound of music came down to me. I must believe that the plan was working exactly.

The street door was slightly ajar; the tapers in the entrance were out—thank God for the economies of the time—the counting-house door, just inside the entrance, was scarcely open, just unlatched. The laughter and the scraping of fiddles were louder here: voices came from the big room above, and from the kitchen—officers and men alike were being kept busy. I pulled the counting-house door: the sneck gave a rattle that made my heart leap to my throat. The fiddlers played on; the sounds from the kitchen did not change. I slipped into the room, sank on to the floor, and, waiting for my body to grow calmer, settled myself to stay there until the guests departed. I was not safe yet: not really home.

Chapter 21

The waiting was not easy. I was home at last, but in that home were officers and men whose duty it was to hunt out people like me. True, they had no idea of my presence and the last place they would think of looking for a Royalist fugitive would be in the house of a trusted Roundhead. But suppose one of them decided to come into the counting-house? It was useless to tell myself that there was no conceivable reason why he should. Or suppose one of them, when leaving, stumbled against the door and it burst open? This danger was a real one—I could be sure that they would have been given plenty to drink. I fumbled my way to the door again and felt where the lock should be. There was a key on the inside: Thomas Trumbell had thought of everything. I turned it gently, then eased it out of the lock, tiptoed back to the farthest corner between the great oak coffer and the desk, and settled down again to wait.

I felt safer now, but the next hour was one of the longest I have ever spent. It was warm after the autumn air outside. I durst not move for fear of making a noise. The stench of my clothes sickened my stomach. Most of all, I was so nearly home that it was hard to be patient.

At last, suddenly, the music stopped. There was a thud, followed by a commotion. Heavy steps ran across the room above me. A door was flung open, and Thomas Trumbell's agitated voice shouted, 'Alyse, Alyse, come quickly!' He clattered half-way down the stairs and shouted again, 'Alyse, hurry, your mistress is taken ill.'

I heard Alyse's old feet mount the steps, making as much haste as they could. There was a brief hush, then she gave a loud cry and burst into sobs. After that I could hear only agitated murmers. I strained my ears. Was everything going according to plan? Then came heavy feet on the stairs, then voices in the entrance, just outside the counting-house. This was the most dangerous moment of all. But the guests were departing, hurriedly, and not only the evening's guests but also the men lodged in the house.

'You'll have to lie on the floor,' said one voice, 'but you'll not mind that, for the one night.'

There was a tremor in the voice that answered. 'Nay, anywhere will do, so long as it's not in this house: may God have mercy on it—and on her. Has the city not suffered enough, without a visitation of the plague?'

The plan had worked. The house had been cleared of Roundheads. Moreover, it was not likely to be visited, now, by Parliament men in search of Royalist fugitives. Whether the town authorities decided to try to hush up the appearance of the plague until the Fair was over, or not, we could count on a day or two's isolation.

I had to force myself to wait for the signal that it would be safe for me to come out of my hiding-place. At last there came a light scratching on the door as a hand felt for the sneck, and a familiar voice whispered, 'Ralph, Ralph, are you there? It's safe now.' It was Alyse. For a moment I was disappointed that it was not my mother or Emmet. But only for a moment. In nightmares I had tried to get to my home again: in dreams I had never left it. Now that I was once again in the house in the Close, I was suddenly glad to delay for a little, only a little, the meeting with Emmet and my mother, partly perhaps to savour the prospect a few minutes longer, but mostly, I think, because I was afraid that reality might be less satisfying than dreams.

When the door of the counting-house was unlocked, Alyse set down on the big chest in the entrance the candle she was carrying and came to me with arms outstretched. Too late I remembered the state of my clothes. Her indignation was so sudden and so comic that I could not help laughing out loud: I suppose my nerves were on edge. After a moment when she did not know whether to be vexed or not, she laughed too. Thomas Trumbell came quickly downstairs to remind us that we could spoil everything if our laughter were heard by neighbours or by passers-by. This sobered us very quickly and Alyse led me away for cleansing, clucking over the state of my clothes, 'Scotsman's, only fit for burning anyway,' as if I were a boy come home from school with a torn jerkin and had never been away. We went to the warm kitchen, fragrant from the evening's cooking: it seemed to have grown much larger while I had been away. My mother and sister were not there either. My stepfather—I could call him that at last—had come with us and he told me that my mother and Emmet were waiting for me upstairs in the Great Chamber, just in case one of the officers had forgotten some of his possessions and came back. 'Not that it's likely he would, not to a house where he thinks there's plague,' he said, 'but it's best to be on the safe side.' Kit had been right: there was no one as good as Thomas Trumbell at thinking of possible trouble. And I was thankful for it.

I submitted to Alyse's ministrations and mingled reproaches and affection more patiently than had that other Ralph Cole in that very same place, scarcely more than two months before. But I began to fret inwardly with impatience, for the precious moments were going by and I did not know how many I would have before I must leave again.

'Nay, Alyse, nay; let be,' Thomas Trumbell said at last. 'The lad's mother is waiting.'

I went out of the kitchen, through the dark hall to the stairs to the Great Chamber. I saw Thomas Trumbell lay a restraining hand on Alyse's arm to make her wait with him. Now nightmare, dream, and reality were coming together at last. A last rush of shyness made me hesitate. What could I say? How could I begin to say I was sorry? Then my foot was on the stair. The door of the Great Chamber was opening and candle-light streamed through. How short the stairs were, after all, and how easy to climb, and at the top were waiting Emmet and my mother, and there was no need for words at all.

POSTSCRIPT

Ralph Cole had only one day at his home in the Close before he was smuggled on board a collier which took him to Antwerp. There he was to stay with his uncle and learn the overseas side of the coal trade, until better times came and he could return home to Newcastle. But King Charles did not come to terms with Parliament and was executed; it became obvious that Ralph's exile would be for a long time, maybe for ever. Then Ralph realized that since his wanderings after the fall of Tynemouth Castle his heart had not been able to reconcile the two sides of his experience of the coal trade. He went to Padua to study medicine.

He was able to keep in touch with his family through letters. So he learnt that in the next winter after he left England, Parliamentary forces made a determined and partly successful effort to clear out Royalists still hiding in the Border country and to put down the mosstroopers once and for all. Jackie Armstrong, his brother, and Nessie were all killed in an attack on Elsdon. Adam was one of a small party that escaped into the hills and was never heard of again.

Kit Sanderson's association with Thomas Trumbell was profitable to them both and Kit eventually became a hostman. The measure of his success was his marriage, two years after the death of Ellen, to Emmet, Ralph's sister. It was a sensible hostman's marriage, but Ralph believed that Emmet was happy in a sober, quiet way.

Archie Reede's story was the happiest of all: he worked with Kit for a while, then went back to Elsdon to help to build a new way of living for those of his people who were left.

Then, at the Restoration of Charles II, Ralph was at last able to return to Newcastle, after twelve years of exile; he found it colder and greyer than he remembered. His mother and Alyse were no longer living, and Emmet and Kit and Thomas Trumbell, kind though they were, were busy with their own lives. So Ralph went back to Italy, which he had grown to love, and took up again his work among the poor of Padua. There he married and there were born his children, and the grandchildren to whom this story was told.

GLOSSARY

ADIT — A gently-sloping horizontal opening by which a mine was drained. Some adits were only four feet high and eighteen inches broad.

ARVAL — A funeral feast; a wake.

BANDOLEER — A shoulder-belt with cartridge-loops.

BENCH — Also called a room or a board. The place where a single miner cut into the coal face.

BOARD — A section of the coal seam.

COCKET — A document sealed by officers of the Custom-House and delivered to merchants as a certificate that merchandise had been entered and that duty had been paid.

'COLOURING' COAL — A member of the Hostmen's Guild who sold, as if they were his own, the coals of a non-member was said to 'colour' the coals. This was forbidden by the rules of the Guild, and the member would be liable to a fine, or even loss of membership. Nevertheless, it was done at the time of this story, and the practice increased as time went on.

COMPANY OF HOSTMEN — A guild in Newcastle upon Tyne which originally received strangers (called hosts)

180

who came to buy coal and other commodities. In the seventeenth century the hostmen controlled the selling and exportation of coal.

CORVER   The name given to the man who made the corves or wooden baskets in which coal was loaded to be taken to the surface. Usually the corves were made of hazel twigs.

CRACKET   A low wooden stool.

GARDE-ROBE   A privy.

KEEKER   The man who inspected the coal before it was sent to the surface.

KEEL   A flat-bottomed vessel used on the Tyne for loading colliers. It carried about twenty tons of coal and had a crew of four. The skipper was in charge of the keel. Another keelman steered by means of a large oar, called the swape. The remaining two keelmen propelled the vessel by means of long poles, called the puys. There was also a square sail that could be used.

HEWER   The miner who cut out the coal.

HINNIE   A polite form of address to either sex.

HOGGERS   Coarse woollen stockings.

HURRIER   Also known as the putter. The man who filled the corves and dragged them to the shaft. Sometimes the corves were loaded on to four-wheeled carriages known as trams. The barrowman pulled and the putter or hurrier putted or pushed behind.

LAYSTALL   A place where refuse and dung were laid.

MARRA	A workmate; a friend.
MIDDEN	A refuse heap.
MOSSTROOPER	A bandit or raider belonging to the Border country between England and Scotland; also known as rievers.
SALT-PAN	A shallow vessel in which brine was evaporated in salt-making.
STAITHES	Derived from the Anglo-Saxon word Stathe and formerly applied to single fixed dwellings or to places on the banks of rivers, where merchandise was stored, and at which vessels could lie to receive it.
STYTH	Also known as choke-damp. A gas now known to contain a mixture of carbon-dioxide and nitrogen, and so called because its presence in large quantities could choke or suffocate all those coming into contact with it.
SURFET	Also known as fire-damp. A highly explosive gas (chemically known as carburetted hydrogen or methane) released from the coal during mining.

TITLES IN THIS SERIES